DEATH ON THE ELEVENTH HOLE

Recent Titles by J M Gregson from Severn House

Lambert and Hook Mysteries

DEATH ON THE ELEVENTH HOLE
GIRL GONE MISSING
AN UNSUITABLE DEATH
AN ACADEMIC DEATH

Detective Inspector Peach Mysteries

TO KILL A WIFE
A LITTLE LEARNING
MISSING, PRESUMED DEAD
A TURBULENT PRIEST
WHO SAW HIM DIE?
THE LANCASHIRE LEOPARD

DEATH ON THE ELEVENTH HOLE

J. M. Gregson

Severn House

This first world edition published in Great Britain 2002 by
SEVERN HOUSE PUBLISHERS LTD of
9–15 High Street, Sutton, Surrey SM1 1DF.
This first world edition published in the USA 2002 by
SEVERN HOUSE PUBLISHERS INC of
595 Madison Avenue, New York, N.Y. 10022.

British Library Cataloguing in Publication Data

Gregson, J. M. (James Michael)
    Death on the eleventh hole
    1.   Lambert, Superintendent John (Fictitious character) - Fiction
    2.   Hook, Sergeant Bert (Fictitious character) - Fiction
    3.   Police - England - Lancashire - Fiction
    4.   Detective and mystery stories
    I.   Title
    823.9'14 [F]

    ISBN 0-7278-5814-9

Typeset by Palimpsest Book Production Ltd.,
Polmont, Stirlingshire, Scotland.
Printed and bound in Great Britain by
MPG Books Ltd., Bodmin, Cornwall.

To Frank and Yolande Hughes,
faithful supporters

One

Kate Wharton thrust her hands deep into the pockets of her thin, short coat. It would be May tomorrow, but there was a sharpness in the evening air which reminded her that it was still only spring. There might even be a frost before the night was out.

She was on the edge of the city of Gloucester, but this part of the city was largely deserted at nine thirty as darkness dropped upon the roofs. It seemed darker and more threatening within these streets, where shuttered shops towered above her, and she longed for the movement which even a breath of wind would bring to the place. The silence and stillness oppressed her: she felt as though she was observed by a thousand mocking eyes.

The cold and the quiet made her resolution seem pointless, the course of action she proposed quite hopeless. Kate tried to thrust such negative thoughts from her mind, to assure herself of the logic of the course which she had now planned for her life. She knew that she was right, but she would have been glad at this moment of a close friend or a relative she could trust to assure her of just that.

Kate was pleased to reach the lower end of Westgate Street and pass into the older part of the city. The buildings were lower here, and she glimpsed the great bulk of the Cathedral, rising against the dark blue of early night as it had done for centuries. She thought for a moment about the medieval workmen who had raised these stones, and seen the same stars as she now saw sequinning the sky behind the tall tower. Then she turned left and back into the starkness of the present, as the Cathedral and its outbuildings disappeared abruptly from her view.

Kate Wharton was making for a public house which was in the area of the old docks. This was a tourist area now, with money spent on modernizing the old warehouses into antiques centres and museums; it was a cheerful, even a bustling place by day, with parties of schoolchildren on educational visits and holidaymakers looking for diversion in the summer. But it was silent and almost deserted now, and the only building of which Kate was conscious was the prison on her left. She was relieved when she glimpsed the lights of the pub.

She was glad to be at last among people, even people she did not know. She took a deep breath and looked at her watch as she went up to the front door of the hostelry. It was coming up to a quarter to ten.

There were not many people in the place on this Monday evening, so that Kate had no trouble in securing a table for herself as she carried her half of draught cider away from the bar. For a time, no one took any notice of the white-faced girl who sipped anxiously at her drink and kept glancing nervously towards the door. But this was not London or Manchester: a girl on her own still attracted attention in a pub. Kate Wharton had opened her coat in the warmth of the bar, and her thin cotton skirt exposed rather too much shapely leg for her own good.

'Another of those, is it, m'dear?' The man was perhaps thirty, with a pencil-thin moustache that he probably thought made him look racy. He spoke with the local burr of Gloucestershire or Herefordshire. He had a leather jacket, sharp brown eyes, an empty smile, and too much confidence. Kate was only just in time to snatch her glass away as he reached for it.

'No, thanks. I'm waiting for a friend.'

He slid his jeaned buttocks on to the bench beside her. 'Nearly ten o'clock. He's stood you up, m'dear. Shouldn't leave you in a place like this, a defenceless girl like you.'

She noticed that he didn't say a nice girl or a pretty girl, the way they usually did. She didn't like that 'defenceless'. Kate said stiffly, 'I'd rather be left on my own, if you don't mind.'

'Oh, but I do, you see. Mind, I mean. When I see a young girl on her own in a place like this, I regard it as my duty to protect her. To take charge of her, even. Let me fill that up, m'dear, and we'll see how it goes from there, shall we?' He let his gaze wander insolently down over her small breasts to her waist and hips, to the hem of the skirt she had pulled at automatically with his arrival, then up again to the triangle of her crotch, where he let it stay.

It was insolence without words: the action of a man who was going to have what he wanted from her, whether she delivered it willingly or not. But Kate had dealt with his sort before: you grew up quickly when you came from her background. She sat upright, looking far calmer than she actually felt. 'Look, I've told you politely once that I want to be left alone. Now I'm telling you less politely. Piss off! Perhaps you'll understand that.'

He allowed his predatory smile to develop into a short, mirthless laugh, so that the thin line of his moustache stretched above a full set of teeth, which were white but uneven. 'Things are getting better all the time! I like a bit of spirit in my women. Bit of spunk, as you might say. I can see we're going to get on quite well together – if you play your cards right, m'dear.'

It was the first hint of a threat, and with it the smile disappeared. Kate Wharton looked beyond him to the thinly populated pub. No one was giving any attention

3

to this conversation in the corner. She repeated, 'I said piss off. Now go, will you! I'm not in the mood.'

He glanced around, following her gaze to the rest of the big, low-ceilinged room, gathering as she had that no one was interested in a little spat between a couple in a corner. It was that kind of pub. And she was this kind of girl: he was confident of that. He finished his beer and gave her his charmless smile again, edging it with a touch of menace. Then he moved his fingers to caress the thigh which he had now convinced himself had been exposed to attract him. 'You know you want it, m'dear – you wouldn't be here unless you did.'

At that moment, someone she could not see, round the corner of the bar, in the invisible arm of the building which had once been a separate room, called out, 'Anyone for a game of darts? We only need one.'

Kate Wharton was on her feet in an instant, thrusting aside the clumsy arm which reached for her. 'Here I am!' she called, breaking into a clumsy short-stepping run, lest any other volunteer should get round the corner to the game before her.

The boys with the darts were about her own age, surprised and then pleased to see a girl coming forward to join them. 'Your arrows, then!' said a tousled-haired lad of about twenty. 'You're with me, love.' He had a northern accent which she couldn't place more precisely than that; she found it reassuring after the local burr of the man who had tried to force himself upon her.

She came to the oche, toed the line primly with the point of her small foot, and delivered the darts carefully at the board. She was out of practice, but she knew she was not hopeless at this game. When you had grown up as the only girl in a street filled with boys, when you had ventured into pubs long before the legal age for such pleasures, you were bound to know a little bit about darts. She was delighted to get a double and set the scoring in motion with her second dart. It was received with delighted and exaggerated acclaim by her new companions.

Thereafter, she did not score heavily, but she didn't miss the dartboard altogether, as the lads had half-expected a woman to do. Each minor success was greeted with noisy delight by the young men around her. Her late tormentor sat at the side of the room, watching with a sardonic smile, waiting for the moment when this diversion would end and he could make his next move. With his pencil-thin moustache and his slicked-back hair, he looked like a thirties gangster on one of those old films she had watched on daytime television as a lonely child.

But Kate wasn't worried about him. She knew that by the time this darts diversion was over, there would be another man waiting for her, the man she had come here to meet. He was late already. But he was a man who could afford to be late. He wasn't like that pathetic package of lust who waited hopefully on the fringe of the room. The man who had arranged to meet her here was a man who really frightened her.

They were halfway through the game of darts when she saw him at the bar. Characteristically, he had arrived there without her noticing his entry. He was watching her, without troubling to disguise the fact. If he was surprised to see her playing darts with these boys, he gave no sign of it. He sat on a stool at the bar, sipping his whisky and water appreciatively and studying her movements as she threw the arrows at the board. It did not improve her performance.

Partly as a result of this, she and her cheerful partner lost the game. The boys asked her to carry on playing, said they would shuffle the sides, but she shook her head with a forced smile and moved to join the man at the bar. He acknowledged her presence with a nod, indicated with an

5

even briefer movement of his head that they should move to the corner of the room where she had gone to await his arrival half an hour earlier. She caught sight of her late pursuer slinking out of the pub with a sour smile as she moved back to the spot where he had approached her.

Flynn didn't offer to buy her a drink, didn't offer even the briefest of greetings. He sat hunched within an anonymous navy anorak, with the collar turned up high enough to meet the quarter-inch stubble around his face. Only his cold grey eyes had any sign of animation, and they now fixed themselves upon a Kate Wharton who was trying to still an unexpected trembling in her limbs. Flynn sat waiting for her to speak, and she had no idea where to begin.

'I want out!' she said abruptly. It had come on a rush of breath, so that even the brief three monosyllables left her breathless. It was a declaration of the very nervousness she had planned to conceal.

He looked at her without expression, delaying his reply for a second or two to savour her apprehension. 'You can't,' he said simply, finally.

'I can and I must. I'm only twenty. I can build something else. I can have another kind of life. I can—' She stopped, interrupting the list of things she had told herself when she made this decision. They didn't seem to carry the weight here that they had held for her alone in the bedsit.

Flynn took another unhurried sip of his whisky, ran the tip of his forefinger round the edge of the glass. He had heard all this before, from other girls like this. 'You can what? Go back on the game? Pick up where you left off as a tart?'

'No! Well perhaps, if I need to, for a while. But that doesn't matter to you. I'm just telling you that I'm not going to be a pusher any more.'

'"I'm not going to be a pusher any more."' He took advantage of the fact that there was no one within ten yards

6

of them to mimic her high, nervous tones. 'Get real, Kate! No one walks out on us! Not me, not the blokes above me in the chain! And certainly not you!' He allowed himself his first smile, to show his contempt for the absurd idea.

Kate mustered her remaining nerve, tried hard to thrust it into her voice as she said, 'That's ridiculous! I want out and I'm getting out. I never grassed in the past, and I won't now. No one will find out anything I know. In any case, I don't know anything worth having, anything the police might—'

'You know about me, for a start. And that's enough. I'm not putting my life in the hands of some little tart who doesn't know her own mind for two minutes together. You can forget that, darling!' His smile showed his teeth for the first time as he gave her a wolfish grin.

Kate continued desperately: 'I'll move away from here. No one will ever know I was even involved. You can get someone else to go round the pubs easily enough, to pass on the supplies you provide. There's a big demand for horse and smack and ecstasy, and with the quantities of Rohypnol I've been shifting, there's plenty of money in it for someone. You won't have much difficulty—'

'No!' The word came like a gunshot. Flynn was a man not used to argument, not happy enough with words to want any discussion. 'I'm telling you, not asking you, you silly little bitch! You stay with the job. God knows, it's paying you well enough.'

Well enough for me to get out before it destroys me, thought Kate. She said, 'I'm going. There's nothing you or anyone else can do about it.'

Flynn looked at her with contempt. 'And where are you going to get your own supplies, you silly cow, if you finish with us? These things don't come cheap, you know. You do know, better than most.'

That was true enough. Even her ten per cent made her

a handsome living. Easy money, if you didn't mind the trade. She tried to look back into the thin, evil face with the same contempt he was showing for her. 'I don't need it. I've never needed it. Not the hard stuff. I've never used anything stronger than pot. Not on a regular basis.'

He made a sudden grab, seized her thin wrist, used his other hand to wrench back the sleeve of her dress, tearing the cotton a little in the process. The flesh was unmarked. A light blue vein ran upwards from the wrist until it disappeared into the white, almost translucent skin of the forearm, but there was no sign of the scratches or the puncture marks which Flynn had expected. He did not merely drop the arm: he flung it towards the floor, so that she had a taste of the strength and frustration which lay within this dangerous opponent. He was a man not used to opposition. He snarled, 'So you don't inject. That proves nothing, Miss Wharton!'

It was the first time Kate had ever heard him use her surname, and it was hissed with an irony which sounded an alarm in her ears. She wanted to terminate this last meeting, to be away from him, from the pub, from Gloucester itself. 'I told you. I've never done more than dabble with hard drugs. I'm not a user. You can't keep me that way.'

Flynn stared at her through narrowed eyes. Most of the pushers he recruited were users of Class A drugs, hooked on heroin or cocaine. It meant they could not cease to peddle the drugs with which he supplied them: their feeble and spasmodic attempts to get out of the trade foundered on their own dependency, on their own need for the very drugs they dealt in. He cracked the whip and they fell back hopelessly into line in return for their regular free supplies.

This white-faced, determined girl apparently did not have this weakness. She was standing up to him, telling him she could leave him without coming back for her supplies like a whipped mongrel bitch. It would be the worse for her in the end: his masters wouldn't let her get away with simply walking out on her job as retailer at the business end of the trade. Bad for discipline, that would be, if the word got round. But it would reflect badly on him if they had to take steps like that. He needed to protect his own back. And to do that, he needed to convince this silly young cow of the danger she was inviting.

Flynn went to the bar, got himself a double whisky and topped it up with the same quantity of water. He kept his eye on the stubborn, pallid girl at the table, ready to intervene if she made any attempt to leave. She stared down at the round table in front of her like one frozen in a nightmare. He brought a half-pint of cider back with him, banged it down hard on the table in front of her, so that the top inch of it slopped on to the table and down on to the thin cotton dress.

Kate felt the liquid cold and wet against the top of her thigh, seeping with an insidious tickle into the soft flesh around her crotch. Still she did not move, as if any sign of discomfort or annoyance would be a confession of weakness to this hard man with his narrow, despicable mind. What she was doing was the right thing: she clung to that through her confusion and misery like a lifebelt in the vast cold of the sea. She said in a voice which seemed to belong to someone else, 'I'll leave the area altogether. You won't hear any more from me. And neither will the police.'

Flynn found himself struggling again to marshal any reasoned argument. He dealt in threats and force, and until now they had always been enough. He was obscurely aware that he needed to convince this girl that there was no future in what she planned, but he found it difficult to summon up the right words to do it. He said dully, 'It's not an option. They don't allow it.'

She caught the frustration in his face, and drew from it a little surge of strength. 'They will this time. They won't have a choice.'

At that moment, as if to support the sudden optimism she had felt, two large men came into the room and walked slowly to the bar, leaning with elbows on it as they waited for their pints and surveyed the big, half-empty room. Plain-clothes coppers; Kate wondered if anyone in the pub was deceived by their too-bright sweaters and their too-clean jeans. She certainly wasn't: one of them had arrested her eighteen months ago for soliciting. She wondered if he recognized her as he took in unhurriedly this exchange he could not hear between the unshaven man and the young girl in the corner of the saloon bar.

That didn't matter to Kate. They were allies now, in this situation, and she must use them. She forced a smile at the intense, sinewy man on the other side of the small round table, stood up, pulled her coat around her and fastened it. 'That's it, then. I don't suppose we shall meet again. Goodbye, Mr Flynn.' She invested his title with the same sneer he had given to hers a few minutes earlier.

He thought for a moment she was going to offer him a handshake, but she turned abruptly away from him. He made a desperate grab at her wrist, missed it, and dropped his arm to his side as he saw the copper watching him.

Kate Wharton passed the policemen without checking her step, without offering them any sign of recognition. Then she was through the door and gone, without once interrupting the brisk pace of her walk.

Flynn knew he couldn't follow her without exciting the interest of the two big men at the bar, who were watching him now without any attempt to disguise their interest. He made a show of sipping his whisky without haste.

That silly girl had just signed her death warrant.

Two

Superintendent John Lambert sniffed the air like a boy
newly released from school. There were not many
better places to be on a bright May evening than the golf
course at Ross-on-Wye. He teed his ball on the tenth tee,
fixed his eye on it like a malevolent hawk, and despatched
it through the tunnel of trees and down the very centre of the
fairway. Then he tried not to look surprised by this result.
A beautiful spring evening had just become perfect.

His pleasure was in no way diminished when Sergeant
Bert Hook, a fearsome cricketer but still a self-confessed
novice in this infuriating game of golf, pulled his ball deep
into the left-hand trees that his chief had just so trium-
phantly avoided. 'Right shoulder coming over the ball,'
he said to Hook. 'Common fault, but very destructive.'
Lambert strode off down the fairway towards his distant
ball, his back seemingly unaffected by the glance of molten
fury which Hook cast upon it.

Bert found his ball and hacked it savagely out of the
trees to a point some way behind the spot where the
Superintendent's ball had come to rest. A cloud of energetic
flies followed his sweating figure and buzzed gently around
his head, as though preparing to mug him. He mused once
again upon the paradox that John Lambert, by some way
the finest copper he had ever worked for, could be such a
patronizing prat on the golf course.

Bert still needed a wooden club for his third shot.

Lambert seemed about to offer advice, so he swung the club savagely before he could receive it. The result was predictable, but in a strange, desperate way quite gratifying. He thinned the ball savagely, and it flew like a bullet, waist-high towards the man in front of him. For a not unpleasing moment, Bert Hook thought that it might pass right through Lambert. Instead, curling like a lethal banana, it narrowly missed the cringing John Lambert and disappeared comprehensively into the trees, this time on the right of the fairway. Hook regarded his visibly shaken opponent with some satisfaction. 'Give you this hole, John,' he said with a grim smile. He set off with his trolley towards the eleventh tee, with head held high, a model for all in his acceptance of the cruel blows of adversity.

John Lambert could have picked up his ball and followed, having won the hole, but he could not resist hitting a second shot after his perfect drive. He got his ball almost to the green, chipped it to six feet, watched his putt twist round the hole instead of into it, and mimed a theatrical anguish with his arms in the air. He found the gesture was wholly wasted on his sergeant, who had ostentatiously turned his back and was watching the movements of a vivid green woodpecker in the woodland beyond the green.

'Should have had a par from that drive,' said John Lambert with a rueful shake of his grizzled head, as he joined Hook on the eleventh tee.

'Bloody stupid game! Don't know why I let you talk me into it!' growled Hook constructively.

'Because you're now too old for cricket and you still need the exercise,' said Lambert equably. He found it easy to be philosophical about the charms of the game when he was striking the ball well.

'Some bloody exercise! You don't have to be an athlete for this. The fat boy in *Pickwick Papers* could manage golf, for all the athleticism it demands.' His comparisons had taken on a literary bent since his Open University studies.

Lambert resisted the comment that the game seemed at present to be demanding more of Hook than his highly tuned athleticism could deliver. Instead, he tried encouragement: his wife, a successful teacher, assured him constantly that the carrot was a more successful teaching aid than the whip. 'You're really the ideal build for this game, you know, Bert. Five feet eleven and powerfully built. Very few good golfers are as tall as me, you know.'

Hook looked up into his chief's lined, experienced face. 'I bloody know all that. That clever bugger Peter Alliss is always going on about it on television. In between encouraging poor mugs like me to take up the game. Runs a lot of people into needless expense, that twerp does, pretending the game is so easy. All right for him: he started as a boy. He doesn't know what it's like to get hold of a club for the first time in your forties, silly sod.'

Lambert had teed up his ball at the beginning of this diatribe. He waited patiently for it to subside, feeling a little as King Canute must have felt, for he knew that his sturdy sergeant could keep up this strain indefinitely. Taking advantage of a silence, but knowing it might only be a pause for the drawing of breath, he swung hastily at his ball.

Too hastily. His ball sliced low and right, just clear of the trees, but not long enough to reach the corner of the dog leg on the eleventh. Hook observed its progress with every sign of pleasure. 'See what you mean now about the right shoulder coming over the ball,' he said cheerfully. 'You took it back all right, but you were a little quick in the downswing, I think.'

Lambert tried hard not to be irritated by this recent tendency of his protégé to impart advice instead of merely receiving it meekly and striving to implement it. He found that he slammed his driver back into his bag with a vehemence which was altogether too revealing.

Hook had already teed up his own ball. Lambert began to offer a useful tip, but Bert stilled him with a lordly raising of his palm which brooked no argument. Then he swung his clubhead easily through the ball and sent it bouncing well past the corner of the dog leg, to a point where he would need only a short iron to reach the green, a display of competence which was even more annoying to his mentor than his refusal to listen to advice.

Bert Hook made a stately progress to his ball, with his sturdy frame erect and his nose a little in the air. But pride, as so often in this infuriating game, went before a fall. He swung easily and confidently at his 7-iron to the green – and topped the ball horribly. He watched the ball unbelievingly as it flew low and ugly to his right, barely clearing the ditch which runs thirty yards in front of the eleventh green at Ross and clinging precariously to the far bank of it as it ran towards the hedge by the road. He affected not to hear Lambert's cheerful, 'Snatched at that a little, didn't you? Lucky not to be out of bounds on the road!' as he stamped angrily after his ball. The activity which had been a subtle test of skill a moment earlier was transformed in an instant back to a bloody stupid game.

John Lambert managed to play his third shot into the middle of the green, but his comment on this modest triumph was stilled by the sight of Hook standing stock still to his right, looking down not at his ball but at something within the ditch beyond it.

There is something in the pose of a man frozen into immobility by what he sees which communicates itself to others around him, and Lambert knew in a moment that this was something serious, something which stretched outside the comfortable confines of men at play. He left his clubs and went slowly, almost reluctantly, through the long shadows thrown by the setting sun to stand beside his companion.

His arrival seemed to galvanize Hook into action. He moved cautiously to the side of the ditch. The thing within it had blocked the slow flow of the filthy drainage water, so that it was now half-floating, half supported by the sides of the narrow ditch. There was water beneath a patch of soiled green shirt, lifting it above the shoulders, making the figure seem bloated, obscene, inhuman.

The corpse lay on its back, but the face and most of the body had been hastily covered with reeds and coarse grass. Bert Hook knew better than to touch what he now knew must be human remains. But he turned and lifted the grass gently, almost reverently, with the club he still held in his hand. He did not attempt to alter the position of the body, but he lifted the covering just enough for them to see the face.

It was the face of a young woman, perhaps in her early twenties. It looked in death untroubled, almost serene. That was the worst thing of all.

Three

Superintendent John Lambert had a strange feeling as he took the familiar turning and drove his old Vauxhall Senator into the golf club car park.

This place had always meant pleasure for him, always been a relief from the tedium and the occasional horrors of work. Now that was no longer the case: he eased the big car up to the long wooden Terrapin building which had already been set up as a murder room. 'Any identification yet?' he asked Inspector Chris Rushton, who was recording the steadily accruing information on his computer.

'No, sir. She certainly hasn't been reported as a missing person locally. We're checking the national MISPA records, but that will take some time.'

Normally there would have been surprise at a superintendent taking such a direct role in a murder investigation. The modern CID superintendent is an office man, keeping an overview of the various strands of a murder inquiry, deploying the considerable resources of a serious crime investigation in what he sees as the most effective way. But Lambert was a dinosaur among senior detectives, a man who insisted on being directly involved in a murder hunt himself. He was nearing retirement now, and perhaps seen as too old to change his ways; more importantly, he got results, and his superiors were prepared to indulge eccentricity in a man who did that.

Lambert strolled down the course to the spot on the

eleventh where Bert Hook had discovered the body on the previous night. The fairways were busy on this bright spring morning, and it seemed strange to him to be walking here without a golf club in his hand. The birds sang joyously in the oaks and beeches and chestnuts on his right, as if they too were glad to be rid of the heavy rain which had ushered in May in the Wye Valley. High white clouds moved slowly across an intense blue sky. The unfurling leaves of the forest trees were fresh and moist, with that bright intensity of green which only spring growth seems to offer. It seemed a very odd place to be conducting a murder investigation.

The area where they had found the corpse was still cordoned off with plastic tape, and two constables were conducting a detailed search of the area around the ditch. But the body itself had been lifted into its plastic 'shell' and removed in the van policemen call the 'meat wagon' for its post-mortem examination. By this evening Sergeant Jack Johnson and his Scenes of Crime team would be away, having gathered whatever information they could from this innocent-looking place. Golfers were already playing the hole, giving the police activity on their right curious glances as they passed. By tomorrow, there would be nothing here to indicate the sinister discovery of thirty-six hours earlier.

Lambert looked at the gleam of water in the bottom of the ditch, which had been concealed by the girl's body on the previous evening, and said to Johnson, 'Anything interesting for us, Jack?'

They were old hands these two, of a similar age, and with a healthy respect for each other's professional skills. If Johnson said there was nothing more to be discovered at the scene of any particular crime, he was invariably right, for he had evolved his meticulous methods over many years, had even contributed modestly to the SOC procedures laid down in the police manuals. He shook his head. 'There's not a lot for us here, John. Forensic might come up with a bit more from the clothes, but I doubt it. You've got a careful man here.'

They spoke automatically of the killer as a man, simply because it was overwhelmingly statistically probable. Lambert nodded slowly; he had disciplined himself over the years not to expect easy pickings at the outset of an investigation. 'Was she killed here?'

'No. The duty surgeon confirmed that when he certified death last night.'

'Cause of death?'

'Almost certainly strangulation. The pathologist said he might be able to give us a little more on that after the PM.' Johnson moved over to the hedge. 'She was almost certainly killed somewhere else and brought here in a vehicle to be dumped. You can see where someone has pushed his way through the hedge and pulled it back afterwards.'

Lambert nodded, looking at the bits of twig and new leaf which the constables were collecting from the spot with tweezers and putting into plastic bags. Each of these fragments would be examined under a forensic microscope for any signs of fibre from a killer's clothing. 'Any footprints?'

Johnson shrugged. 'The photographer's taken shots of whatever's there. Maybe something will emerge when he does his blow-ups. But I'm not hopeful. Come and look at this.' He led Lambert over to the ground shadowed by the hedge, where sun rarely penetrated and the ground was still soft from the winter rains. Whilst they stood carefully outside this key area, so as not to contaminate it with any indentations of their own, Johnson pointed to what might well have been a footprint. It was smooth at the bottom, indefinite round the edges, with no sign of any useful sole or heel patterns. 'That's the kind of mark you make if you're wearing these,' said the SOC sergeant.

Lambert looked down at the white plastic bags which both he and Johnson wore over their shoes, the addition anyone venturing on to a Scenes of Crime area had to make to their footwear, to avoid contamination of the site and confusion with any marks that might have been left by the criminal or his victim. 'You mean he was cautious enough to put something over his feet before he carried the body through the hedge?'

'That's what it looks like to me, John. Plastic bags are thrust at you everywhere these days.'

Superintendent Lambert was thoughtful as he strode back up the course to the murder room. A cautious killer, who killed when he was ready, hid the body in a pre-determined spot, and took informed precautions with his footwear to disguise his presence.

The bright spring morning seemed suddenly a little darker.

The first suggestion of the victim's identity came not at the murder room beside the golf course but at the police station at Oldford.

Lambert had reported to the Chief Constable, confirmed they had a murder investigation, and relayed to him the scanty details of the crime so far available. He was clearing his desk of other cases when the station sergeant's voice informed him on the internal phone that a Mrs Eastham would like to see him in connection with the discovery of a female corpse at the Ross-on-Wye golf course.

The woman was a thin-faced woman of around sixty – he decided that her lined face probably made her look older than she actually was. Her hennaed hair was grey at the roots and her blue eyes were watery. Long experience told him that she was a drinker, though she seemed perfectly sober at the moment. She looked carefully to the right and left of him as he sat at his desk, as if she feared there might be other presences, even in this small, square room. She looked briefly at him, then down at his desk as she said, 'This girl you've found. I think it might be one of my tenants.'

Though he had no reason to suspect her, Lambert's instinctive reaction was to put her on the back foot. 'No one has released anything yet about the dead woman's age, Mrs Eastham. Can you tell me why you're so sure it's a young woman?'

The watery blue eyes looked up at him then, full of fear, which made him feel a little ashamed. 'I'm not sure, am I? It's just that I thought she might be one of my tenants. Young girl of twenty-one or twenty-two. Might not be her, for all I know. Just thought you should know, that's all.'

There was a strange mixture of apprehension and trucu-lence about this pathetic figure in a mackintosh which was too long for her. Lambert divined that she had been in trouble with the police in her time, that she was no stranger to police stations, but that she was perfectly innocent on this occasion. People like Liz Eastham did not come to see senior policemen willingly when they had anything to hide: their natural inclination was to steer well clear of police interrogation. He looked steadily into the lined, shifty face, wondering why a woman like this had come here today to volunteer information.

Her next words gave him the clue to that. 'She didn't come in to give me her rent on Sunday night, did she?'

He picked up a pen. 'You'd better let me have this girl's name, Mrs Eastham.'

'Katherine Mary Wharton.' She recited it carefully, picturing the words she had written so carefully at the top of the rent book. 'But she called herself Kate. Everyone knew her as Kate.'

'I see. And you're telling me that she didn't come to see you on Sunday night, and that you haven't seen her since. When was the last time you did see her, Mrs Eastham?'

She glanced into the long, alert face on the other side of the desk, then looked down at her knees and furrowed her brow, as if considering the question. She must surely have thought of this before she ventured into a police station, Lambert thought, as he gazed at the grey roots beneath the orange-red hair on the crown of the bowed head. 'Last Thursday, I think. I saw her going out that night. About seven thirty, that would be. But she may have been around since then. I don't spy on my tenants, you know!'

Lambert smiled into the defiant face. 'No one accused you of doing that, Mrs Eastham. It might have been better for us if you did, in these circumstances. But I'm glad you've come forward to do your public duty.'

She looked at him sharply, as if she suspected the irony he had tried to keep out of his voice. 'I 'aven't anything to 'ide, 'ave I?' She dropped for a moment into both the argot and the manner of the petty criminal he was certain she had been in her time. 'When will I be able to let the place?'

So this was why she had persuaded herself to set foot in a police station; the rent she was losing. He had the answer to the question which had puzzled him when she had first been shown into the room. 'If Katherine Wharton is the girl who's been killed, you won't be able to let the room for some time, I'm afraid. Not until a team from here has been over the place very thoroughly.' He watched the apprehension seep into her face as he reached for a second sheet of paper. 'Where do you live, Mrs Eastham?'

'Matthew Street.'

He could picture the houses now. Three-storeyed, with cellars beneath, in terraces which had been going slowly downmarket throughout the century after Victoria's death. With their front gardens concreted over to allow the parking of as many vehicles as possible. Most of them now split into segments for cheap letting to tenants who could afford nothing better. No more than three streets from the place where the appalling Fred and Rosemary West had conducted their ghastly, unthinkable series of murders of young people. The police had not come well out of that grisly carnage, and no policeman could be happy with the thought of it. Lambert looked steadily into the tired, crafty face. 'You let rooms?'

'I let apartments.' There was a pathetic hauteur about her correction. 'I live at the back of the ground floor myself, and I have a little garden at the rear of the house.' This small assertion of gentility was clearly important to her.

'And the rest of the house is sectioned off for lettings?'

She nodded, mollified by his acknowledgement that they were more than just rooms. 'There are four of them altogether, of different sizes. Three of them are single units, and the fourth one is a double.' She spoke the words almost without a breath: it was plainly a spiel she was used to delivering to prospective tenants. There would be a high turnover in a house like hers. Not many people would stay for long – unless the area happened to suit their special requirements.

'And which of these did Katherine Wharton occupy?'

'Kate. We all called her Kate.' It seemed suddenly important to assert the last threads of individuality that clung to the girl she was now sure lay dead, the girl whose body was perhaps at this moment being cut up like the carcass of a farm beast. 'Kate had the double. On the first floor. They have a big living room and a bedroom each.'

'Who do, Mrs Eastham?' He kept the surprise out of his voice, delivered the question as if it were more dull routine. But this flatmate, not the landlady, should surely have come forward with the news of her missing companion. She would have been the first one to know that Kate had not come home, the first one to feel the pangs of anxiety about that.

'Kate and Tracey. Tracey Boyd. They pay their rents separately, but they occupy the place together.'

'So when did Miss Boyd last pay her rent?'

'Last Friday. Regular as clockwork, they are, with their rents. Tracey every Friday, Kate every Sunday. They know I don't stand for any nonsense.' She folded her arms suddenly, as if asserting herself as the stern landlady.

'And Tracey didn't mention on Friday that Kate Wharton was missing?'

'No. She may not have been missing, of course, on Friday. I told you, I last saw her on Thursday, but Tracey may have seen her after that.' Liz Eastham's instinct was to place the burden of answering on to this as yet anonymous contemporary of Kate's, to extricate herself as quickly as possible from police questioning.

Lambert nodded. 'We shall have to see her in due course, if the girl who's been killed is indeed Kate Wharton.' He opened a drawer in his desk and picked out the facial photograph of the corpse that he had selected for identification purposes. 'Do you think that this is her?'

Liz Eastham's thin fingers trembled a little as she took the photograph, handling it as carefully as if it had been a sacred relic. She looked at the serene, lineless face, with its eyes closed in the peace of death, for two long seconds. Then she said, 'Yes. That's Kate all right.'

She would have liked to weep a little as she handed the picture back to the superintendent who would search for her killer: it seemed the only proper thing to do.

But the tears would not come.

Four

Detective Sergeant Bert Hook had broken the news of death to many distraught parents in his time. He tended to be selected for this task for two reasons. The first was that he had a natural empathy with people caught in such dreadful circumstances: beneath his weather-beaten village bobby exterior, there was a ready response to the distress he saw. The second and more important reason for CID purposes was that he was a deceptively acute observer: his stolid bearing concealed an instant feeling for any reaction which was false, any facial expression which betrayed the mind behind it.

It was a valuable quality whenever there were suspicious circumstances surrounding a death. With three-quarters of all murders in the area committed by members of the family, even a mother was suspect at this stage of an inquiry. Hence the reason for a CID officer as well as the uniformed policewoman on this grim mission.

The woman who opened the door to them seemed to have no premonition that they brought bad news. She said to Hook as he offered his warrant card, 'You didn't say you'd have company when you phoned, Sergeant,' and stood looking down with a slight smile at the trainee woman constable who stood behind him.

Julie Wharton proved to be a woman in her early forties, with a rather square, carefully made-up face framed by a helmet of skilfully cut dark hair. She wore a bright green

24

sweater and dark green, almost black trousers. She looked for a moment longer at the heavy figure of Hook in his light grey suit, then at the uniformed girl who seemed scarcely old enough to be out of school. Then she led them through a narrow hall and into a neat living room. There she turned to face them, so abruptly that they were arrested suddenly in the doorway of the room. Householder and visitors stood awkwardly facing each other, scarcely three feet apart.

Hook said, 'I think it would be better if you sat down, Mrs Wharton,' and promptly sat down on the sofa himself, with the uniformed girl beside him. Julie Wharton hesitated, and he thought for an instant she was going to question his presumption. Then she sat down and said with a little sigh, 'You'd better tell me what this is all about, Sergeant Hook.'

He had expected her to show alarm when he asked her to sit down, to catch some intimation of the awful news he brought. But still she behaved as if she had no apprehension of bad news. Hook cleared his throat and said formally, 'I believe you have a daughter, Katherine Mary Wharton,'

For the first time, her face clouded, with his use of the girl's full name. 'My daughter is Kate Wharton, yes. Is there something wrong?'

Hook reached into the inside pocket of his jacket, thought for an awful moment that he had forgotten the picture, then felt the corner and drew the photograph of the dead girl carefully forth. 'Yes, I'm afraid something may be very wrong. Do you think this might be Kate?'

She took the picture from him, looked for four, five, six seconds silently at the black and white photograph of the unlined, serene face with the closed eyes, whilst her audience watched anxiously for any sign of distress. Then she said in a perfectly even voice, 'That's my daughter, yes. That's Kate.'

Still she looked at the picture, and still she gave no sign

of hysteria. Hook was well aware that grief had many ways of manifesting itself, that an outwardly dull response could well be one of these. He said gently, watching the square, still face carefully, 'That is the picture of a girl found dead on Ross-on-Wye golf course on Monday evening. I'm very sorry, Mrs Wharton.'

Still she did not look up from the face of the dead girl. 'She looks very peaceful. As though she was just asleep.'

Hook tried hard not to think of what might be happening to that face at the autopsy, thrust from his mind the image of the skin being peeled back to allow the removal of the brain from the skull. He said, 'Do you know where Kate has been during the last few days?'

She looked up at him at last. 'No. We're not in touch much nowadays. She has – had – her own life to live.'

Hook nodded imperceptibly to the young woman at his side, and she came in on cue with, 'Perhaps I could make us all a nice cup of tea, Mrs Wharton. We know this must be an awful shock and—'

'I don't need tea. I'll get you one, though, if you want one. I don't like other people working in my kitchen.' Mrs Wharton rose abruptly and left the room without waiting for any confirmation.

Hook said quietly to the WPC, whose first suspicious death this was, 'Go in there and provide whatever support you can. Don't talk to her unless she invites it. And let her make the tea herself if she wants to. Performing simple actions can be better therapy for some than drinking sweet tea.'

He listened for the sound of conversation from the kitchen, for the sudden shriek of pain and outrage which might crack that carefully made-up mask of a face and allow the agony of a bereaved mother to burst out. He heard the sounds of crockery being assembled, but no noise of muted conversation.

Julie Wharton allowed the young WPC in her crisp new uniform to precede her with the tray as she re-entered the room, but that was the limit of assistance she allowed to the girl. She handed them plates, offered biscuits, poured the tea with a steady hand. Hook, who had accepted the offer of tea to prolong his study of this strange mother, found himself wishing that they could be out of the house and free of this strange, unreal atmosphere.

He made small talk, but this disturbing host replied in monosyllables. The girl beside him, who had been prepared for a harrowing experience, for holding a tearful and distraught older woman in her young arms, could offer nothing in the face of this polite denial of the conventions of grief.

Bert Hook eventually said, 'We'll need to talk to you about your daughter in due course, Mrs Wharton. But not now. Superintendent Lambert will probably wish to speak to you, later in the week.'

She nodded. 'You'll need someone to identify the body, won't you? I'll come with you now, if you like.'

Hook, who had been wondering how to broach the subject, thought rapidly. The body would need to be tidied up after the pathologist's cuttings before it could be presented to a relative. He said, 'That's very good of you. But not now. Perhaps later today, or tomorrow morning. I'll give you a ring about it.'

Julie Wharton stood on the steps and watched them go with her hands at her sides, smooth and immutable as an Inca goddess. Hook would have given a great deal to know what happened to that face once the door was shut upon the world outside.

Lambert was getting ready to leave the police station at Oldford when the call came.

'Chief Constable here, John. Could you come up to my

office for a moment, please?' There was an odd diffidence in the usually confident voice, but what may be framed in the form of a polite request is a command when it comes from the CC, even to a superintendent.

Douglas Gibson had known John Lambert for over twenty years, had indeed been instrumental in allowing him the freedom to operate like a superintendent from a previous age, one who attended the scenes of crimes and questioned suspects himself as investigations developed. Gibson was a silver-haired, handsome man, who preferred to keep his finger on the pulse of a small efficient country police force rather than move on to the larger city post he could undoubtedly have commanded.

He was unusually constrained on this Tuesday afternoon, as the sun poured into his office on the top floor of the building. There was a tray with china cups and saucers and a tray of ginger nuts. 'I'm elevated to VIP status today,' said Lambert, as he sat down in front of the huge desk.

Gibson smiled wanly as he came round the desk and sat in one of the armchairs beside the senior officer in his CID section. He was a man who was good with words, who could use the guarded phrases of diplomacy with the public as easily as he could fire bullets at officers who fell below the standards of efficiency or integrity which he demanded. Yet now, with a man he had known and respected for years, he did not know how to begin.

'How are things at home, John?' Gibson's words sounded feeble in his own ears.

'Not bad. Christine's had no recurrence of the breast cancer, and the heart bypass seems to have given her a new lease of life. She's teaching again, and enjoying it. A part-time post: five half-days a week.'

'I'm glad to hear it!' Gibson was relieved to be able to say something genuine. His own daughter had been taught by Christine Lambert, a quarter of a century ago, and still spoke of her with great affection. 'She has a lot to give, your missus. How old is she now, John?'

With that question, Lambert knew suddenly what this was all about, as clearly as if it had been written on the Chief Constable's forehead. 'You want to talk to me about retirement, don't you?'

Relief suffused Gibson's features before he could stop it. 'I should have known you'd be on to me before I could come out with it. Yes, I'm afraid that's why I asked you up here.'

Lambert didn't know what he thought, could not even estimate his own reaction to the news, beyond a ridiculous pleasure that he had taken the initiative himself in raising the word. His tongue seemed to run on without any permission from his brain as it said, 'Well, I'm fifty-eight already, as you no doubt know from the staff files: three years beyond the normal age of retirement.'

'Yes, I do know that. It was I who made out the case for your service to be extended. Not that the authorities needed much persuasion, in your case, I'm happy to say.'

'But now it's time to go.'

'Not as far as I'm concerned. You know I'd keep you on as long as you were prepared to stay, if I was allowed to. But our masters think they know better. They're wrong in this case, as they so often are.'

Lambert swallowed a bite of biscuit, forced himself to take a mouthful of his cooling tea. 'I can't grumble. I've had a good innings.' He grinned sourly at the feeble metaphor.

'If they extended service on the basis of results, you'd be here for another twenty years, John.'

'Thank you for that. But sometimes the outsider's view is the more objective. It's probably time I went.' He felt anaesthetized, as if he were listening to someone else making the appropriate modest responses.

'Not from the standpoint of crime detection it isn't, John. But maybe from your own perspective, it is. You must have thought about retirement.'

'I have. Often.'

'You've earned it.'

'Thank you. I'm not sure I'm quite ready for it, but I'm sure I'll adjust.'

'You and me both, John. I've been wondering how I'll cope with it, these last few years. They say you adjust to it more rapidly than you expect. That you wonder within a few months how you ever found time to go to work.'

Lambert was suddenly resentful of the ubiquitous 'they', with their easy consolations and their vapid platitudes. He said with a doleful smile, 'Well, at least I've got my rose beds going strong. The copper's traditional retirement occupation.' He loved his garden, yet its pleasures seemed to him now an evasion, a retreat from the harsh reality of the human scrapheap.

Gibson said, 'It's the usual thing: a central directive that has to be implemented by everyone, whatever the individual circumstances. They won't even look at special cases, with people who've already had extensions to their service.'

'And I thought they were expanding the police service, taking on more people to combat the increase in crime.' Lambert found himself quoting the government's recent announcement, and hated himself for this first hint of bitterness.

'They're expanding the service all right. But they also want to improve the career prospects of those already in. Senior ranks over a certain age are being pushed out to make way for promotions.'

Lambert managed a genuine grin at last. 'It's a reasonable enough policy. We'd both have been pushing for it thirty years ago.'

'And the old farts would have been keeping us firmly in our places! Oh, you're right, John, it's a reasonable enough policy. But there should be room for exceptions, for a special case to be made out in particular circumstances.'

'You know as well as I do that the policy would disappear under hundreds of applications, hundreds of "special cases", if they allowed room for appeals.' Lambert smiled, suddenly conscious of the irony in his arguing for the very axe which was cutting off his working head.

Gibson stood up. He was genuinely sorry to lose this most successful of his policemen, but he was enough of a tactician to know when to call a halt. 'I'm very sorry, John. You know it wasn't my doing. If I can find any loophole in the directive, you know I will.'

Lambert nodded, scarcely hearing him now, conscious only that he was being dismissed, that he wanted to get out of the room with whatever dignity he could summon. He turned at the door, not wanting to ask the question, but knowing that he must be certain of the details of this bombshell. 'How long?'

Douglas Gibson, who had been relaxing in the thought of an unpleasant task completed, looked apologetic again. 'Your next birthday, I'm afraid. They won't go beyond that. Everyone here will want to say goodbye to you, but we'll talk about all that later.'

Lambert nodded. 'Three and a half months, then. Better go and get on with the job. Tidy things up for the new man!'

He was immediately sorry for that cheap parting shot, felt himself diminished by it as he went carefully back down the familiar stairs. He stopped for a moment on a deserted corridor of the floor below, looking out over the lush green spring countryside of Gloucestershire beyond the stone buildings of the old market town. He felt like screaming at this cheerful, uncaring world, for its beauty and its strong new growth, as he had done when he heard of Christine's cancer five years earlier; as he had done nearly thirty years ago, when they had lost one of their children in infancy.

He had forgotten he had ever known that feeling until it renewed itself now. He told himself that he should be ashamed, that retirement was not to be compared with any sort of death. Yet it was for him, he was sure, a kind of bereavement.

He went back into his office, trying to shrug away his melancholy in a determination to get on with his work. There was a murder to occupy him: the death of this girl Kate Wharton. He had always felt a little guilty about the way he relished a murder investigation, though he knew that it was only the hunter's instinct which every successful CID officer must have. There wasn't much to go on yet in this one. But this hunt more than any other must conclude with an arrest.

This might be his very last murder.

Five

T he next morning was overcast, with enough nip in the air to remind everyone that this was still an English spring, even if it was the ninth of May. Bert Hook picked Mrs Julie Wharton up at nine o'clock to take her to identify the body of her murdered daughter.

She was ready for him, so that she had no need to invite him to re-enter the quiet house. But DS Hook had looked up the row of small rear gardens as he turned into the road, and his observant policeman's eye had noticed a line of washing behind the house of Mrs Wharton. A line which contained men's underwear, socks and shirts. So it seemed that this enigmatic woman probably did not live alone. There was a man about the place, though she had volunteered no information about his presence on the previous day.

She wore a dark blue coat above sheer nylon tights and navy shoes, dressed as decorously as if she were bound for a funeral. But there were no signs of distress about her appearance or her bearing; she was as carefully made up as on the previous day beneath her neatly cut dark hair. She said, 'I could have driven there myself, you know. There was no need for you to collect me.'

Bert smiled. 'We like to give what little support we can. This can be a distressing experience.' He wondered if she realized that he was curious to detect how she really felt about this dead daughter, that he did not accept the emotionless front she had presented on the previous afternoon.

Whatever her thoughts, she revealed little about herself on the way to the mortuary, and Bert was too conscious of the stressful nature of the task ahead to press her to speak. She volunteered the information that she had not seen Kate for 'at least a month' before her death, and he deduced, though she did not put it into words, that there had been little intimacy between mother and daughter.

He wondered when and how the relationship had gone astray. Bert, a late entrant to the lottery of marriage, was the father of two boisterous boys and no daughters, but he had always thought that the mother–daughter bond was the strongest of all ties, the one most likely to survive the traumas of adolescence. So he presumed that the quiet, contained woman beside him had been close to the dead girl at one time, that something quite serious must have occurred to fracture the relationship.

But he gained nothing from Julie Wharton, who behaved as though the coolness between mother and daughter, which she had tacitly suggested, was the most natural thing in the world. He glanced sideways at her as he turned into the neat, aseptic surrounds of the mortuary and parked the police Mondeo beside the only other two cars which were there. If she felt any inner turmoil at the approaching ordeal, she gave no sign of it. She stared straight ahead at the brick walls of the low building; the profile of her strong, square face might have been cast in bronze.

The attendant outside the identification room was more nervous than she was. He was not used to meeting such composure in the close relatives of the corpses which were the centre of his working world. He fretted a little over the completion of the familiar forms, showed her unnecessarily where she would sign in due course, stumbled a little as he explained the procedure. Hook could have sworn there was a little impatience in the nods with which Julie Wharton acknowledged his instructions.

It was Hook who asked her the final routine question. 'Would you like a moment or two alone before you see the body?'

'No.' It seemed almost an afterthought, a gesture towards convention, when she said, 'I'd like to get this over with as quickly as possible, please.'

They had done a good job in the pathology lab in tidying up the corpse, using the girl's plentiful hair to disguise the stitching at the front of the skull where the skin had been drawn back to allow entry to the head. The woman before them looked younger than her years, almost girlish in the absence of even the smallest of lines from the face. She looked, as Julie Wharton had said when she studied the photograph of the dead woman on the previous afternoon, almost as if she were asleep.

The emotion which had been held in check in the mother for almost an hour did not burst through with the revelation of the corpse. Perhaps, Bert Hook thought with a chill, it did not even exist.

The mortuary attendant drew the sheet back carefully from the dead face, careful not to expose the livid marks about the neck which gave the clue to how she had died. Bert Hook, standing unobtrusively behind the mother, did not hear the gasp of horror or distress he had expected. There was a slight tensing of the square shoulder blades in front of him, but no sound. Then Julie Wharton's voice said calmly, 'Yes. That's Kate. I'll sign those identification papers now.'

She was, he decided, the calmest of the trio in that cold and silent room. She refused the offer to allow her a few minutes alone with all that remained of her daughter, turned away as the still face was covered again, signed the papers, refused the offer of a hot drink, and was back in the police Mondeo within five minutes.

Neither of them spoke for some time as Hook drove her carefully home. Eventually he said, 'It's a distressing business, always, the identification, but it has to be done.'

'I understand that.'

He searched hard for some consoling words. 'When it's a road accident death, it can sometimes be really harrowing.'

He wanted to bite his tongue off at the crassness of this, but all she said was, 'I can imagine it would be.'

He gave up any attempt to offer consolation and concentrated on the road. Just when he had decided she would not speak again, she said, 'What about the funeral? Do I have to make arrangements?'

A strange way of framing the question, he thought. Most relatives wanted to know when they could conduct the ritual of mourning which was the last gesture to the dead: this woman spoke as if it were some kind of imposition. He said, 'I'm afraid you may not be able to arrange the funeral for some time, Mrs Wharton. There'll be an inquest, and even then the coroner probably won't release the body for burial or cremation. That usually has to wait until – well until –'

'Until there's been an arrest?'

'Yes.'

'Why's that?'

'Well, the defence lawyers have a right to ask for a second post-mortem by their own pathologist, if they want to dispute the findings of the first one.'

'I see.' She nodded thoughtfully, seemingly not at all upset by the idea of the body being stored for months and then opened up again.

When they drove into the row of neat, anonymous houses, she was out of the car before he could ease his

36

own solid frame from the driving seat. She thanked him for the lift, as politely as if they had been out shopping.

It was only after she had shut the door of the house behind her that he realized she had still not asked how her daughter had been killed.

It was DI Rushton who took the call, sitting at his computer in the murder room beside the golf course. 'They gave me the number at Oldford police station. Said you were the person I should contact.'

The voice was confident, used to the phone, educated, without the local accent of Herefordshire or Gloucestershire, certainly without the thicker rural burr of the Forest of Dean. Rushton put on the interested but neutral voice he reserved for members of the public. 'What can I do for you, sir?'

'Well, it's probably nothing.' The opening any CID man had heard hundreds of times. 'But I thought it was something you should know about.'

'Who are you, please?' said Rushton politely, his hands poised over his computer keyboard.

'Sorry! My name is Jason Gillespie. I'm a Catholic priest. I run a care centre in Gloucester, St Anne's House.'

'I know it, Father. To be strictly accurate, I know of it, and something about the work you do, but I've never been there. Well, you think that you have something which relates to our investigation, or you wouldn't have been put through here.'

'Yes. It may be nothing, as I say, but I thought I'd better report it. You never know quite how much attention to pay to addicts.'

Rushton took a swift decision. 'I think I'd better come over and see you. This would be better done face to face.'

'I must confess that I'd find it easier, if you could spare the time.'

'I'll just get someone else to take over here. I'll be over early this afternoon.'

There was always time, when the crime was murder. Always resources: even the bureaucratic straitjackets of overtime were not powerful enough to constrain murder investigations. And for an inspector fiercely conscious of his career prospects, the chance to unearth an addict who had strangled Kate Wharton was immensely attractive.

DI Rushton left the murder room at Ross Golf Club and arranged for a detective sergeant to take over temporary responsibility for assembling the information coming in from house-to-house and other enquiries. At the same moment, the captain of another golf club, eight miles away at Oldford, was concluding his Wednesday morning four-ball game with his friends.

They knew each other well, these four men. All of them were just over sixty and recently retired or semi-retired. Richard Ellacott had his own accountancy business and still went in two days a week to deal with a few of his old accounts. Since he was this year's Captain of Oldford Golf Club, he was appearing in the office even less frequently, in order to give full and conscientious attention to his duties at the golf club.

In truth, these were not onerous. Oldford was a small club, less prestigious and less demanding of its Captain's time than a club like Ross. Ellacott could probably have joined Ross, but he was comfortable at Oldford, and his golf was mediocre enough for him to recognize that he might not have enjoyed the longer and trickier course at Ross. He had played there often in club matches, and had never been able to command the straight hitting which the course demanded.

And if he was honest, he knew he would never have become Captain there, whereas his long membership at

Oldford had more or less ensured that the honour would come his way in time. He was enjoying the captaincy of this smaller club, basking in the kudos it gave him as he moved around the clubhouse and spoke to members, displaying what he thought of as an easy panache among the ladies when he played with them in mixed competitions.

Yet this morning, when they had showered and changed after the golf, he was not his normal ebullient self with his companions. He was first at the bar and bought his round of drinks, but the normal banter among the four who had played seemed to pass him by. When they twitted him about the two-foot putt he had missed to win the sixteenth, he grinned weakly and failed to come up with his normal unprintable riposte. It seemed to his partner, who had lost money by his Captain's omission, that he scarcely remembered the moment. Which for any golfer anywhere would have been mighty unusual.

Richard Ellacott must have had something on his mind, but no one was certain what it was.

Even his greetings to members coming into the club were abnormally muted. He responded rather than taking the initiative, as he usually did. At his own table, he paid his pound on their modest wager without his customary complaints about the handicaps of the opposition. And he switched to halves after the first pint. Something was clearly preoccupying the Captain.

His companions shrugged the thought aside in the noisy hilarity which surrounded their after-match drinks. They came here to enjoy themselves, and they usually succeeded. If Richard Ellacott was a little out of sorts today, they weren't going to let that stop them savouring their beer, toasted sandwiches and exuberant conversation. You might not be able to play golf like Tiger Woods, might even in your sixties be on the downward slope of golfing achievement, but you could enjoy this part of the day more than ever, especially when you could savour the thought that other people were at work.

Had they been a little more observant, they might have noticed that their Captain was watching the progress of the *Oldford Gazette* around the lounge bar. The club had it delivered every Wednesday, just as it took the *Daily Telegraph* each morning for the benefit of its members. Today far more members than usual picked up their local rag and gave close attention to its front page, where the body which had been found on the neighbouring course at Ross-on-Wye got full coverage.

When his companions had left and the clubhouse was almost empty, Richard Ellacott sauntered over to the bar, where the steward had just put down the paper before going away to connect up another keg of lager. He glanced carefully around to make sure he was not observed and then took the *Oldford Gazette* away to an armchair in the corner.

He read the coverage of the murder very carefully. The police had not yet released a picture of the dead girl, but there were large photographs of the spot where she had been discovered on the eleventh hole at Ross golf course, with quotations from members and speculation about how long the body had been lying there before it was discovered. Foul play was definitely suspected and enquiries were proceeding, but there was as yet no sign of an arrest.

The police knew nothing yet, then. Or nothing they were prepared to release to the local newshounds. The slightly smudged print gave an impression of great haste, as if the paper had held back its deadline to include the tremulous prose with which it greeted this local sensation. Richard Ellacott went over everything twice, finding it curiously consoling that there was no mention of his name anywhere in these hastily compiled columns.

He had not expected anything, of course. Perhaps the police would never even come to see him. He drove home to his wife with a dozen greenhouse carnations, and gave her conversation more than his usual attention.

Six

C hris Rushton locked his car carefully outside St
Anne's House in Gloucester. The big, shabby house
was in the red-light district and he was glad that it was
daylight now. He was relieved also as he went into the
place that he was in plain clothes. The people he saw
moving about in the place were the sort who would have
shown instant hostility to a police uniform.

It was easy enough to distinguish the voluntary helpers
from the clients the place was trying to help. An elderly
woman was listening patiently to a white-faced, shifty-
looking man who was almost six feet tall and looked as
if he weighed less than nine stones. She directed Rushton
to Father Gillespie's room without a curious glance and
turned back to the man who looked as if he would not live
out the year.

The inspector found the priest kneeling in prayer with
an emaciated girl, who was probably eighteen but looked
fourteen. Rushton stood awkwardly outside the open door
until they had finished. Father Gillespie must have been
aware of him, but he did not divert his attention from the
girl. He said as they stood up, 'You were fine today, Annie.
You ate enough to keep body and soul together. And we've
just given a little food to your soul, haven't we? I think
you'll find Eileen downstairs. Have a talk with her and see
what she feels about things.'

The girl nodded, then retreated through the door without

a word, keeping her front towards the priest like one retreating from a royal personage. She would have backed into Rushton if he had not stepped quickly aside. Once in the passageway, she turned without looking at the inspector and moved away in a rapid shuffle, with the heels of her slippers never leaving the ground.

The priest was small and wiry. He wore baggy, stained trousers and was in shirt sleeves; a dog collar sat oddly above an old sleeveless pullover. He looked at the girl's retreating back for a moment, then shook his shoulders and made a visible effort to change roles and speak to Rushton. 'Jason Gillespie.' He held out his hand. 'Father Jason Gillespie, as you can see from the dog collar. I tried to do without it, when we started this place, but our guests like it. They like a clergyman to wear his badge, so that they know where they stand. It's saved me from being thumped, more than once. Old habits die hard, even when life gets desperate.'

Chris Rushton accepted the firm handshake, already after the briefest of views filled with admiration for a man doing good work he knew he could never have done. 'You said you had something to tell me,' he prompted awkwardly. 'Something connected with the murder of Kate Wharton.'

'That's her name, is it? Poor girl.' There was something more than conventional regret in the phrase.

The priest was probably about forty, but he looked older because, despite a determinedly cheerful face and bearing, there was an infinite sadness for the fallibility of human nature in his wide brown eyes. He said, 'I'll need to tell you a little about the way we operate here, so bear with me. We aim to get our visitors off the streets and into eventual detoxification. We provide accommodation, a meal together at one o'clock each day, a day-centre for those who want to visit but not stay here. We tend to get people who haven't any sense of belonging – most of them from adolescence onwards. We try to give them the family environment they don't have, a feeling of trust and respect.'

'Are most of your clients – sorry, visitors – young people?'

'About half and half. We try to separate young people from older users. They are more reclaimable. But we measure success in a different way from the world at large. If someone this week has only taken cocaine three times instead of seven, that is an achievement we applaud. If someone accepts a detoxification programme and sticks to it, that is a triumph.'

'So most of your visitors are drug addicts.'

'Most, but not all. Some are young people who've spent virtually all their lives in the care of the social services, others are no longer in contact with their families. They tend already to be petty criminals. But some are just unable to cope with the deal life has given them. Annie, whom you saw leaving just now, nearly died from anorexia. Someone carried her here from a squat.'

The priest's enthusiasm rose as he spoke about the work of the centre, but Chris Rushton had a feeling of moving further and further out of his depth. He was full of admiration for people who did work like this, but he had joined the police force because he had a passion for order. All policemen had to play things by the book, and Chris found that an advantage, not a restriction. Lambert had spotted a strength in him when he put him in charge of the administration of serious crime cases: Rushton felt most at home filing information and cross-referencing on his computer.

Now, looking at the work of St Anne's House, he felt the panic all of us feel when we contemplate good work we could not possibly achieve ourselves. He took a deep breath and said, 'And you feel that one of your visitors might have strangled Kate Wharton and dumped her body on the golf course?'

The old-young, experienced face above the dog-collar clouded. 'I'm not sure I'd put it as strongly as that. It's more that I don't know what to think. Let me explain. The boy I'm talking about is Joe. I don't even know if that is his real name: it was the one he gave us and stuck to, and we never pry. Joe was an addict. Cocaine first and then heroin. I think he'd have been dead before he was thirty, if the progress of his addiction hadn't been arrested.'

'But it was.'

Father Gillespie nodded, his face brightening a little at the recollection. 'We can't claim all the credit. He says there was a girl involved.'

'Kate Wharton.'

'I don't know. I think it might have been.'

'Father, you have to understand, this is a murder inquiry. You must tell me all you know, even if it comes from within the confessional.'

The priest almost laughed aloud. 'There was nothing like that involved. We don't even ask about religion, here. If the question is raised, it comes from our guests. Joe never raised it.'

'So give me the full story.'

The priest sat down and put his hands together; even the act of sitting still seemed to be an effort for this constantly active man. He nodded three or four times, but not at DI Rushton; it was as though he was convincing himself once again that he should speak about this. 'Joe presented himself here about two years ago. He was brought in by another boy. He was tooting – smoking heroin – every day, and sometimes snorting and injecting as well. He was stealing to support the habit and spiralling rapidly downwards. He stayed here for a little while.'

'And you were able to get him off the heroin?'

Jason Gillespie smiled at the drastic over-simplification of six fraught months in a young man's life. 'Not completely. And not me. I put him with people who were already kicking the habit, people who had gone through the sickness and diarrhoea and all the other humiliations of reform, and come back here to help others. Eventually Joe listened. He registered as an addict and got his supplies at the medical centre. The first and the biggest step towards getting rid of addiction.'

Chris Rushton tried not to show his impatience with this earnest elf of a man. This Joe might be the murderer they sought, revealed by Detective Inspector Rushton on the first real day of the investigation, without any help from the vast police machine of a murder hunt, without the famous intuition of bloody John Lambert. 'So where is Joe now, Father?'

'I don't know. He stopped coming here about a year ago. At first I thought he might have slipped back into his old ways, but other lads who came in here said he hadn't. He came in once more about six months ago, told me he'd got a girl, that he was going to take the cure course, that he was going to be all right. He looked a lot better, but we take nothing for granted; we've seen too many people slip back to the depths.'

'But something must have happened since then, or you wouldn't have rung me this morning.'

'Yes. Joe turned up here unexpectedly last Monday afternoon. He was in a bad state. He'd been on the heroin again. I think it was a one-off. I think he's kicked the habit, but under stress he'd smoked a bit of horse again.'

Chris tried not to show his impatience. Father Gillespie might be concerned about the reversion of an addict he thought he had reclaimed, but this sounded more and more like his man. Whether the violent little sod had kicked back into heroin was a minor matter, in the face of a murder charge. 'What did he say to you which made you suspicious, Father?'

'Nothing, at the time. I didn't know about the death of this young girl, then. Joe was raving about the row he'd had with his girl, about the awful mistake he'd made. He wasn't very coherent, because of his emotion and the horse he'd smoked. I didn't press him for information, just tried to calm him. But when I read about the discovery of this body, I had awful thoughts about Joe. He shouted the girl's name at me when he was in tears. I'm sure it was Kate.'

They stood staring at each other across the shabby room, the priest aghast at the revelation he had finally prised from himself, the inspector trying not to show his rising excitement. Chris kept his voice even as he said, 'Where is Joe now, Father?'

'I don't know. I haven't seen him since Monday. I wanted him to stay for a meal, but he disappeared and—'

'What's his address?'

'I don't know. It's one of our rules that we never press the people who come here for information. They have to trust us. If they choose to—'

'Is there anyone around who would know where he is now?'

Jason Gillespie thought furiously for a moment, weighing his role as priest and the man in charge of this refuge for derelict lives against a crime more serious than anything even he had come across before. Murder won, as it had to in these circumstances. He produced an unexpected grin as he said to Chris Rushton, 'How are you with washing up, Inspector?'

'Well used to it. I live on my own.' For just an instant, the divorced and lonely man felt the attraction he would never admit to of a place like this, with its offers of casual camaraderie, of support without commitment.

'Come with me, then.' The priest was suddenly back

on his own ground and confident again. He bustled out of the room and down two flights of stairs, to a large, stone-flagged kitchen with a huge earthenware sink and long wooden draining boards on either side of it. Rushton realized that this must be the original kitchen of the Victorian house, where a head cook had once presided and the servants had gathered to eat and relax.

A man with a string vest above paint-smeared denims was washing crockery and piling it along the draining boards, more quickly than the peroxide blonde woman of about thirty could dry them and stack them on the table behind her. The youth at the sink had the puncture marks on his inner arms and the woman had the livid bruising of her forearms that spoke of drug injections. Father Gillespie said, 'You need help with that, Ally,' picked up a pot towel himself and handed another one to Rushton, who hung his jacket carefully behind the door and donned a glassy smile.

They wiped plates and dishes assiduously for a few moments. Then the priest said, 'Chris is a copper.'

Both of the drug users glanced sharply at the inspector in his immaculate white shirtsleeves, but they plainly trusted Jason Gillespie, who said with a grin, 'The way you two go on, you could do with a friend at the nick!'

Nothing was said for a few minutes. Rushton had the sense not to try to ingratiate himself. He said nothing and waited for the priest to make the next move. Father Gillespie polished a plate assiduously, set it on top of a pile on the table, and said, 'Ally knew poor Kate Wharton, didn't you, Ally?'

The woman glanced at Rushton from watery blue eyes. 'She was a good kid, Kate. It wasn't her fault she had to earn her living the way she did. Going to get the bastard who did for her, are you? Or do toms not count as victims?'

So the dead girl had been a prostitute. It didn't surprise Rushton, but he registered it as another fact in the dossier they were building about the dead girl. An important one, in all probability. 'We'll get whoever did this,' he said, 'however long it takes, Ally.'

He meant it, and his voice must have carried conviction, for the peroxided woman, who was obviously herself a prostitute, gave a nod of satisfaction and went back to her drying. Priest and inspector found themselves spinning out the task to allow the conversation to continue, assessing the diminishing piles of crockery on the draining boards to allow themselves time for the exchanges they needed. After another couple of minutes, Father Gillespie said, 'Joe Ashton was in here on Monday. Did either of you see him?'

The young man and the older woman both said promptly and with some relief that they hadn't been at St Anne's House on Monday afternoon. There was a further interval before the priest said, 'Does either of you know where Joe's living, now?'

Both of them turned abruptly to look at him. They didn't like questions, about themselves or other people like them, and this was a direct one, with a copper standing there beside the questioner. But the trust the priest had built up over the months held. He looked the woman steadily in the face and said, 'This is murder, Ally. We need to give people like Chris our help if they're to find out who killed Kate.'

She looked at him white-faced, then gave the briefest of nods and went back to her drying. It was the man with his back to them and his hands in the grey and greasy water of the sink who spoke. 'The last I heard, Joe Ashton was in a squat in the city. Sebastopol Terrace, I think it was.'

Seven

Julie Wharton had taken the whole day off from the firm in Cheltenham where she worked.

The men who controlled the small firm of insurance brokers were naturally sympathetic to a woman who had lost her daughter in such awful circumstances. She had always taken care that they knew little of her home circumstances. She ran the office and organized the three girls who worked under her with calm efficiency; the men were glad of that, and didn't want to know about how she lived outside the place, as women might have done.

She wondered if there were many other women like her, who found that the ties of blood were very slight. Kate had been all right as a small child, when she had done charming, unconscious things and worn pretty dresses, which allowed Julie to show her off to her friends. And there had been a mild pleasure in her achievements at school, until the trials of adolescence had begun to outweigh them.

But Julie had always been bored by children talk, by those mothers who built their lives around their progeny. You had your own life to lead, and that was difficult enough. If your children couldn't stay at heel, best be rid of them. Certainly once you had a serious row, you might as well split up for good. She had never subscribed to that foolish saying which people quoted so unthinkingly that blood was thicker than water. Once things had been

50

said that couldn't be forgiven, you were much better living apart for good.

She had rather enjoyed the way she had handled herself this morning, with the identification of Kate's body. She had not thought she could be quite so calm about the whole business. She had enjoyed the feeling that that stolid, conventional sergeant was watching her, waiting for the first signs of a maternal collapse, and failing to find them.

She felt a little empty, a little incomplete, with Kate gone. The world seemed starker and bleaker, and she realized now that she had always assumed that mother and daughter would get together again, eventually. But though she wasn't good at analysing her own feelings, she told herself that she was not so very upset. The bonds of parent and child were, to her mind, largely a creation of a sentimental society.

Not at all like those of sex. Sex was a very different, more animal kind of feeling. She knew how strong its ties could be, but she hadn't fully worked them out yet. Perhaps—

The phone shrilled suddenly, startling her in the quiet house, making her spill the tea she was sipping into her saucer. She knew who it would be, what he would want to know.

'No, there's nothing much to report, really. That Sergeant Hook, the one I told you about, came and took me, and dropped me back here afterwards . . . No, of course I didn't . . . You needn't worry, I don't think the poor man found out anything at all. I was perfectly calm. Unnaturally calm, I'm sure, in the eyes of Sergeant Plod . . . Yes, I'm sure the police will come and see me again, but they'll ring first. They handle bereaved mothers with kid gloves, it wouldn't be good public relations if they didn't . . . No. I don't think so. So far, they don't even know you exist . . . Of course they will, in due course, it's their job to find out things. But I don't see why you've any reason to fear them . . . Yes, I'm sure you could come here . . . All right, but I think you're being a bit paranoid . . . Can't wait to see you! It seems a long time . . . I know, but it seems longer. I'll look forward to that . . . And that too, you randy sod! Bye, then.'

She mouthed a kiss into the mouthpiece, then sat looking at it for a moment after he had rung off.

Sex was definitely different.

Chris Rushton was back in the murder room beside the Ross golf course by four thirty. There was a note to tell him that Superintendent Lambert had gone home, but should be contacted there if anything urgent came up. It wasn't like John Lambert, that, not with a murder investigation gathering pace.

DI Rushton, full of the importance of the breakthrough he had made at St Anne's House, felt cheated by this absence. He had been looking forward to demonstrating that he wasn't desk-bound, that he could use his judgement and initiative when the occasion offered. He decided not to ring the chief at home. It would sound like boasting, and he had too much experience of Lambert's gentle irony to risk offering him an opportunity.

He had found the squat at Sebastopol Terrace in Gloucester, but neither Joe Ashton nor anyone else had been there in mid-afternoon, though there were signs of occupation about the place. He logged the information he had acquired on a new file in the computer. Then he looked at what had come in during his absence. There were a few sightings of vehicles on the quiet road by the golf course where the body had been found, but no one yet knew the time when the body had been dumped. There was a note to say that the full PM report would be delivered by hand the next morning.

Chris felt a rather guilty satisfaction in the knowledge that there had been no discovery throughout this busy Wednesday which rivalled the importance of his own contribution.

It was quiet in the Terrapin hut the police had brought here to provide an incident room. Most of the hastily assembled team were out on the leg-work of routine which always occupied the first days of a murder case. Rushton liked it like this. He set about organizing the material which was accruing into the most logical order, trying to ensure by his cross-referencing that any connections which might emerge as significant would not be missed.

He was thoroughly immersed in the work when a voice almost in his ear said, 'Still keeping your nose clean, Inspector?'

Rushton looked up into an unshaven chin, which had a crooked smile and twinkling blue eyes above it and a shapeless sweater below it. For a moment, he did not recognize the face which had appeared unbidden in hideous close-up, not six inches from his own carefully shaved visage. But the twisted, slightly mocking smile gave the identity away.

'Danny Malone!' he said. 'What the hell are you doing here?'

'If I didn't know you better, me old mate, I'd think that didn't sound very welcoming.' The Irish accent, which had been strong twelve years ago, was only just discernible now. He pulled up a chair, sat down and crossed his legs. 'And anyway, it's not just Danny boy any longer. It's Sergeant Malone, of the Drugs Squad.' He thrust out his chest beneath the sweater in mock pride.

Rushton nodded and grinned. 'I heard.' They had trained together, chalk and cheese in temperament, but thrown together by a common suffering as cadets. Rushton had been the model trainee, serious in intent and heedful of all advice, Malone had been the gifted but wayward recruit, full of potential but with a tendency to use his own initiative where the system did not allow for it. He had sailed pretty near the wind at times, but the strain of the chancer in him was allied to a shrewd intelligence, and it was to the credit of the police service that someone had seen his potential. Malone had got into CID very quickly, three years before Rushton made the transition from uniform. But he had subsequently volunteered himself for the dangerous role of an undercover drugs investigator. The combination of high excitement and high risk, which would have undone Rushton in a week, was much to Danny Malone's taste.

This thought passed through both of their minds as they sat looking at each other. So did the thought that it was Rushton, careful and career-conscious, who had made Detective Inspector, while the maverick Malone, who lived his life in danger and took physical risks his contemporary would never have countenanced, had stuck at Sergeant.

They exchanged a few thoughts about the modern police service, savouring the language of old sweats now, throwing in a little professional cynicism to show how far they had left the trainee days behind them. But the common bond of being cadets, at the mercy of the same training officers, was far behind them, and there was little in their personalities to make them soulmates. Danny Malone, who had always found it easy to win the attention, even the devotion, of girls, was still unmarried, despite a string of relationships. Chris gave the briefest of details of his own marriage and divorce, smiled sourly at the suggestion that he was a newly released Lothario among the women of the district.

After an awkward silence Chris said, 'Do you fancy a quick drink? We can go into the golf clubhouse; they said we're welcome to use the facilities.'

Danny glanced down at his soiled jeans and grinned.

'Not dressed for it, am I? This is working dress for me, but I don't think the Establishment of the golf club would welcome me in.' He looked round to make sure that even police ears could not overhear him; secrecy was a habit with him by now, one of the tools of survival. 'Anyway, I didn't come just for a chat, though it's nice to see an old mate getting on so well.'

Chris looked at him closely, but as usual he could not be sure whether there was a touch of irony in the soft Irish voice. 'This is business?' He reached automatically for his notepad, then checked the movement.

Danny Malone caught the action and grinned. 'Record it if you like, me careful old friend. But you'll have to sit on it until you get permission to move.'

Rushton knew what he meant: you couldn't jeopardize the safety of an undercover drugs officer by following up information he had given you. If you charged in with heavy police feet, it might cost him his cover, even his life. 'Is it connected with the death of this girl Kate Wharton?'

Malone nodded. He was suddenly deadly serious. 'It might mean nothing or it might mean everything. Do you know yet that she was dealing drugs?'

'No. I know that she had a boyfriend who was an addict. Or had been: we haven't managed to contact him yet.' Chris yearned to tell him that this was his discovery, that he wasn't just a dutiful, desk-bound automaton. But he was too professional for that. He was being offered new, possibly vital, information and he must get every detail he could.

'I don't know about the boyfriend. But I did know Kate Wharton and I know she was dealing. The usual story, I think: she got the habit and they used that to persuade her to deal. She was fuelling her own use with free supplies in return for dealing. We could have picked her up several times in the last few months, but it wasn't worth it. She might have led us to bigger fish.'

There was no room for sentiment, for normal human emotions such as pity, in the world in which Danny Malone dwelt. He mourned not the pointless loss of a young life but the loss of a contact who might have led him to significant villains. Rushton said, 'You think she might have been killed by one of her drug contacts?'

Malone shrugged. 'You know the score. If she offended the wrong people, she might have been taken out by a contract killer. I'll tell you what little I know, but you mustn't make contact without consulting my super.'

Rushton nodded. 'Understood. I'll pass that decision on to John Lambert.' He realized that he was proud to name as his immediate superior someone everyone in the area knew.

'That's the way, Chris. Let the super take the decision!' said Malone with a grin.

'It's what they're paid for,' said Rushton tartly. He told himself it was childish, but he knew he still wanted the boyfriend he had discovered to be their killer. 'What makes you think this death may have a drugs connection?'

Malone again gave that habitual check over his shoulder to make sure that he was not overheard. 'I was in a pub by the docks last week. Nine days ago now: Monday the 30th of April.' He watched Rushton note the details, then found he had to force himself to go on with the story: secrecy was a part of his being now. 'Kate Wharton was in there. So was a supplier called Malcolm Flynn. He's further up the chain than the girl was; he provided her with her supplies of coke, E and horse. Anyway, they had a row. I wasn't near enough to hear the details, but it looked serious. Two of your blokes came into the pub; Kate Wharton took advantage of their arrival to get away. Flynn made a grab at her but missed, and he couldn't follow her without exciting the interest of the plods, who'd seen the end of their argument.'

'That's it?'

'That's all there is. I didn't see Kate Wharton again. I haven't seen Flynn either, but that doesn't mean he isn't around.'

'We'll have a better idea of exactly when the girl died by tomorrow morning. But we already know it wasn't on that Monday night. She was killed much later than that – around the end of the week.'

Malone stood up. 'If the drugs men chose to eliminate her, they'd take their time. In all probability, it wouldn't be Flynn, unless he acted off his own bat. They'd use a contract killer.'

That awful 'they': the barons behind the worst and most lucrative industry in the world; the men who had transformed a cheerful young Irish copper into this hunted, shabby creature who did battle with them. And into the kind of hero Chris Rushton knew he could never emulate. 'Good to see you again, Danny,' he said. And meant it.

Danny Malone nodded and turned for the door of the temporary building, suddenly anxious, now that his news was delivered, for the anonymity of the dark underworld he inhabited.

He did not shake hands with his old companion, nor look back at him from the door.

'You were planning to go at sixty anyway. This is not really so different, is it, John?'

John Lambert started with surprise at her words. Christine had been watching him through the kitchen window before she came out into the garden. He had stood for two long minutes with the secateurs in his hand, staring unseeingly over the top of the rose bed towards the sunset.

He turned and smiled at her. 'No, it's not very different. But I suppose I was putting off my thinking about retirement until the last months before I was sixty. It's just been thrust upon me before I was ready for it.'

'And you've been told to go, rather than waiting for what you thought of as the natural time.'

'Yes.' As usual, he was surprised by her perception, though he should have expected it by now. 'I feel I've been declared redundant, identified as surplus to requirements, instead of going in my own time.'

'You shouldn't feel that. I thought you said the CC said it was very much against his own wishes.'

'Yes. And I believed him. It was a central directive, he said.'

'So he had no choice.'

'No. And it happens to people every day. People in much worse situations than me. I know that. It should alter the feeling of rejection, but it doesn't.'

Christine was surprised by their closeness now, by his willingness to talk about this. For years when he was younger, he had shut her out from his work, so that they had almost split up because of his fierce, single-minded dedication to it. She slipped her arm through his. 'You helped me through the mastectomy and the heart bypass. I'll just have to help you through this.'

John Lambert was suddenly ashamed of himself. 'There's no comparison, is there? Those were much more serious things. Matters of life and death.'

'You certainly behaved as though they were, at the time, you old softie! But it was a big help to me that you wanted me to survive so much.' She squeezed his arm. 'Come on, show me round our garden. Tell me what's happening.'

He showed her the sea of promising buds on the roses, found for her the two that were already showing colour. They looked at the branches he had layered from their two choice rhododendrons, and decided together that they had rooted. He would need to spray for greenfly some time during the next week, he said, when the exigencies of this Kate Wharton murder case allowed the time.

Once she had him thinking again about the future, she was content to let him lead her from the cool twilight into the warmth of the bungalow. He had the tall man's slight stoop, the stiffness in his movements that she had only noticed in the last year or two. He had a lot of life to live yet, she hoped, but he was ready for retirement. But you couldn't expect him to see that.

She observed his grey head over the *Times* crossword when he thought she was watching television, took care not to be too assiduous in her attentions when she made a drink at ten thirty. They grinned at each other as they left the lounge, and he said, 'I'm lucky really, aren't I, old girl?'

He knew that it was a title she hated, and they giggled as she punched at his ribs in the darkness. An hour later, after they had made love, Christine muttered sleepily into his ear, 'You're right, you old fool, you're lucky. But perhaps I am, as well.' Then she fell quickly asleep.

At half past three, John Lambert was staring at the invisible ceiling, contemplating the empty years ahead with something like panic, and wondering when the dawn would come.

Eight

The post-mortem report on Kate Wharton gave a few new facts, but mainly confirmed what the leaders of the police team already suspected.

Hook had discovered the body on the golf course at 6.30 on the evening of Monday 7th of May. Death had taken place around twenty-four hours earlier – possibly a little less, but the dumping of the body face upwards in a ditch, with the back of both the torso and the lower limbs in two inches of water, made the progress of rigor mortis a difficult factor to compute.

This made the likeliest time for dumping the body the night before it was found, but so far no one had come forward to record the sighting of a suspicious vehicle on the lane which passed the ditch on the eleventh. This ran through the hamlet of Kempley and connected the Newent–Hereford B road with the village of Dymock. It was a quiet, winding lane, which carried little traffic save at the beginning and end of the normal working day.

Kate Wharton had not been killed where her body was discovered. She had been lifted after death; slight blackening around the left armpit and on the back of the left thigh indicated that the lifting had probably been done by one person, though there was no certainty about that.

She had been killed by the application of a ligature around her neck. This was almost certainly a smooth cord or wire rather than a coarse rope, since no fibres had been found on the throat. The wire had been vigorously applied, probably from the rear, and death would have occurred within seconds. This had probably been preceded by a struggle, since there were tiny skin samples and a single hair under the girl's fingernails, which had been retained for DNA sampling in the event of an arrest.

Hook, listening gravely with Rushton as Lambert took them through the report, said, 'It wasn't premeditated, then. Not if they had a fight beforehand.'

'Maybe she just saw the wire and realized what he had in mind,' said Lambert. 'Or perhaps he didn't originally intend to kill her, but found she wouldn't agree to what he wanted. He had a wire or cord conveniently at hand to kill her with. Maybe that was his last resort.'

'What he wanted probably wasn't sex,' said Hook. Looking further down his photocopy of the PM report, he found a few baldly stated facts which no doubt summarized years of emotional encounters. There was no evidence of recent sexual intercourse. The girl was not pregnant, and never had been. But the organs indicated that she had had considerable sexual experience.

Rushton nodded at that point. 'She was on the game, apparently,' he said. He gave his account of what the peroxided prostitute had told him on the previous afternoon, as they dried dishes together in the kitchen of St Anne's House.

Lambert regarded him curiously for a moment, then commended his initiative in visiting the refuge run by Father Gillespie. He knew St Anne's House himself, as did Hook, and wondered what the rather strait-laced, straight-thinking Rushton had made of the place and its occupants. He asked, 'Have we confirmed the address for Kate Wharton?'

'Yes. It's the one Mrs Eastham gave us on Tuesday.

Matthew Street, Gloucester. There's a Scene of Crime team in there now.'

Lambert nodded. 'There's something odd there. The girl old Ma Eastham said she shared the flat with hasn't come forward.'

Rushton pressed a couple of buttons on his computer. 'Tracey Boyd. Yes, she should have been the first one to notice any absence. But she still hasn't been in touch with us. And Kate Wharton's name is carried in all the papers this morning. It was probably in the *Gloucester Citizen* and on the television news last night. We released it at noon yesterday, after her mother had made the official identification.'

Lambert made a note of Tracey Boyd's name and the number of the house in Matthew Street. 'There may be some simple, innocent explanation for that: she might just have been away for a long weekend, or thought that Kate Wharton was away. But Bert and I will need to have a word with Miss Boyd.'

Bert Hook said, 'The mother needs investigating. I've seen her twice, though not for questioning: the first time was to inform her of the death, the second was to take her for the identification, so I couldn't press her much. Either she masks her feelings exceptionally well, or she's very little affected by this death. I can't make up my mind which.'

Lambert looked at him gravely. It was very unusual for the stolid but surprisingly perceptive Hook to be baffled like this. 'Obviously you couldn't probe much, in those circumstances. But we'll need to get to the bottom of how she feels and how much she knows about this death.'

Bert said diffidently, 'There is one thing I noticed. There was no man around on either of the occasions I visited her house: that's hardly surprising, since each time it was during the day. However, she gave me the impression she lived alone, and there was nothing in her living room to suggest a man. But when I went to collect her yesterday morning, there were men's clothes drying on the washing line.'

Lambert nodded slowly. 'There's no surprise that there should be a man around a youngish widow's skirts, whether permanently or temporarily. But as you say, the fact that she seems to be trying to conceal it may have some interest for us. We'll need to check he had no connection with the murder, whether Mrs Wharton likes it or not.'

'Kate Wharton had a boyfriend,' said Chris Rushton suddenly.

Lambert raised his eyebrows. 'And who told us that?'

His DI almost blushed as he explained how he had convinced Father Gillespie that the police must have whatever information they could get from his guests. 'It was the prostitute who told me Kate had been on the game. It was a lad who was washing the dishes, a drug-user, who told me about the boyfriend. Joe Ashton, he calls himself. According to the lad who told me, he lives in a squat in Sebastopol Terrace in Gloucester.'

'Did you check that out?'

'I tried to. I went round to the house, but there was no one there at all. But it is in use as a squat.'

'Perhaps I should leave you in charge more often, Chris. You seem to have brought information tumbling in. Anything else?'

Chris Rushton tried to look modest. 'There is, actually. But it's not necessarily going to be helpful. Not in making an arrest, I mean.'

Lambert thought he had an inkling of what was coming. 'Let's have it, Chris.'

'When I got back from Gloucester, a pal of mine from years back came in here. He's a sergeant in the Drugs Squad now.'

'And he said Kate Wharton was a user.'

'A user and a dealer. And he said she had a row with her supplier. He doesn't know what it was about, but thought it looked serious.'

'When was this?'

'On the night of Monday the 30th April. In a pub near the docks in Gloucester. Six days before she was killed.'

'Who's the supplier?'

'Bloke called Malcolm Flynn. But there's the usual Drugs Squad proviso. We mustn't approach Flynn without prior consultation.'

Lambert smiled grimly. 'We can't jeopardize your mate's cover. We mustn't even risk doing that. But somehow someone's going to have to follow this up, unless we find that this death definitely isn't drug-related. But leave that with me: it's my problem.'

Rushton tried not to look too relieved. 'If some drug baron thinks that Kate Wharton threatened the security of his organization, it won't be much use talking to Malcolm Flynn. He might not even know who killed her, if they brought in a contract killer.'

'But we shall almost certainly need to speak to Flynn, to establish whether that's what happened. If he passed a report upstairs about her, that could have set the process in motion.' John Lambert pursed his lips. 'The time interval between Monday and Sunday is about right, for them to bring in a contract killer and him to size up her situation and his opportunity.'

They were silent for a moment, each of them hoping this was not the method by which Kate Wharton had died, knowing that the possibility of an arrest was slim, if this was one of the anonymous deaths perpetrated by the black industry of illegal narcotics.

They were beginning the process of finding out about the life the dead girl had led, the life she could never tell them about herself. In twenty-four hours, they would know a lot more about Kate Wharton, but she was already emerging as an isolated, vulnerable figure.

Joe Ashton put his head under the cold tap in the old wash-house at the back of the building. It was the only water they had in the squat. When the house itself had been cut off, the water-board engineers had overlooked this long-disused supply, with a pipe coming in directly from the mains. Probably it was too ancient to appear on any of their charts.

His mouth felt like sandpaper and his head throbbed. He shouldn't have tooted that heroin last night, not when he had kicked the stuff into touch for good. But already he could feel the craving again in his brain, sense the throbbing insistence of his veins for more of the same. He knew the score, knew what lay ahead of him if he went after the horse again. You didn't go through the humiliations of the cure without reaching rock-bottom, without learning how terrifyingly easy it was to slip back to that nadir.

Trouble was, half of him wanted to do that. To kill himself with the stuff, if it came to it – and it would. More than half of him wanted out, now. Since Kate, he wanted to cripple his intelligence, to swamp a mind which had returned to logic and reason with a new derangement.

That small part of his mind that was still functioning normally recalled the sickness, diarrhoea and humiliation of his reclamation, the cold sweats as he ground his forehead into the carpet. He knew that he should do something to save himself, put his fate into other hands than his own destructive ones. But where? And what could he do? He had tried going to see Father Gillespie, who had helped him before, who had brought him out of the sewer of despair without once mentioning God. But how could he stay at St Anne's, after Kate? How could he accept help, after Kate? Sooner or later, someone would start asking questions, someone would seek him out and demand to know what had happened.

He heard a sound at the front of the house. Someone was there. A user of the squat, like himself? He didn't know all of them. He had been here for months now, but people came and went. No one asked any questions, which was why he had come here, why he had been allowed to stay.

There was the sound again. Footsteps. You could hear them, because there were no internal doors left in the place. They had all been burned for warmth, during the winter. He wondered how long that presence had been in the house. Perhaps for many minutes, before he caught the sound; his hearing, like his other faculties, was affected by the drugs. He knew more about what coke and horse did to you than most addicts. He had taken the cure, hadn't he?

Perhaps if he stayed out here they would think there was no one in the place and go away, like that smart bloke in the suit had done yesterday. He found himself cowering in the cobwebbed corner of the old wash-house, his buttocks on the damp flagged floor and his head between his bony knees. He clasped his arms across his chest, tried to pull down the tiny sleeve of his T-shirt over the bruising on his arms. The goose-pimples on his forearms reared before his eyes in hideous close-up two inches from his eyes, the hairs rising from them like the limbless trees of a First World War battlefield.

He hadn't felt that the May morning was cold when he came out here. Now he could not control the violent shivering which had taken him over.

If they didn't come into this little brick outhouse, they would scarcely see him through the single window, which was so filthy that it let in very little light. There wasn't much of the door left – most of it had gone for firewood – but that made the place look more derelict from the outside.

Then Joe heard something which chilled his racing, corrupted blood. It was the sound of his own name, called softly through the big, three-storeyed house across the yard.

They were going to find him, he was certain. He heard the name being called up the rickety staircase, then the sound of cautious steps ascending. There was more than one of them. He thought he heard his name again, more distant, echoing from the high ceilings of the upper rooms of the old house.

He could run for it now, while they were up there. He must run for it. He could be over the back wall, through the house in the terrace behind which was also a squat, away into the centre of the city, burying himself if necessary among the other derelicts there. There was safety in numbers, for someone like him.

But when he tried to lever himself up, his right leg gave way like a stick. He tried again, but all he got from both of his legs was a ridiculous, exaggerated, trembling: they were like the legs of a sleeping dog, which were moved only by dreams. He sank back, feeling the damp again on his bottom, shutting his eyes against the nightmare vision of the goose-pimples on the arms he clasped across his chest.

Perhaps they wouldn't notice him, after all. He lost his sense of time. It seemed to Joe, with his head thrust deep into his chest and his arms over his eyes, that it was a long, long time since he had first heard the noises in the house. Perhaps they had gone now. But he mustn't move yet. He must stay here and not move at all, not even a muscle, until he was sure that it was safe. But he felt his limbs trembling, felt that they were moving out of his control. His head was raging and his thirst seemed to be not just in his mouth, but in his throat, reaching downwards into his chest, beginning to dry out his whole body.

'You all right, son?'

The voice seemed to come from a long way away, from another place, another point in time. It had to repeat the question before Joe opened his eyes. 'I said, are you all right, son?'

Two huge figures rearing in the doorway, black and threatening against the blinding light behind them. An immense distance above him. Two-dimensional, black against the white of the light, so that he could see no feature of the side which was turned towards him. They looked more than human in their stature and their menace, so that he cowered even lower, shutting his eyes, waiting for the blows which must surely come.

Yet the voice had been kind. And the contact, when it came, was gentle, though he ground himself further into the damp beneath him at the touch. 'Get up, son. It's no good for you here. You know that.'

Large hands beneath his elbows, arms which were immensely strong as he scrambled up, the grimy bricks of the corner harsh against his shoulder blades. The voice repeated, 'It's no good for you here, is it? Let's go inside.' He nodded, wanting to comply, sure now that they were not going to hit him.

If this was going to be the end, if it was going to be all over for him, so be it. So long as no one was going to hit him, the end would be rather a relief. He moved out of the wash-house, into sun that seemed blinding, almost lost his balance, turned towards the back door of the house, found the broad hand underneath his elbow again, assisting him that way.

There were two stools and a battered upright chair in the kitchen. They set him carefully on the chair and drew the stools up opposite him, watching him carefully, as if he might break into pieces before their eyes. He could see them, now that they were no longer against the light.

The one who had helped him was a burly man with a weatherbeaten face. The other one, the one who had not yet spoken and yet seemed to be studying him so intently, was taller, with a long face, plentiful, tightly curled grey hair and grey eyes which seemed never to blink.

He had expected them to shout at him. Instead, the tall man said quietly, 'Would you give us your full name please?'

'Joseph Charles Ashton. My friends call me Joe.'

'I'm Detective Superintendent Lambert. And this is Detective Sergeant Hook.'

Joe nodded dully and looked at the sergeant, who gave him a small smile, like a teacher trying to draw out the best from a young child. Joe wished his head would stop thumping, that he could control the shaking in his limbs, which was not constant, but came back to convulse him with another bout of trembling each time he thought he had conquered it.

His mouth was very dry now, and his thirst so great that his tongue felt much too large and seemed determined to adhere to the roof of his mouth. He heard a cracked beaker full of water set amid the deep scratches on the table in front of him. The sergeant said, 'Drink, lad, and get a hold of yourself. We need to ask you a few questions.' He watched Joe drink, looked at him assessingly with his head on one side, decided he was not going to fall off the chair, and sat down on his stool.

Joe told himself to be careful, when he heard about questions. These men were coppers, they'd just told him that. And a superintendent was quite high up in the police, he remembered that. He took another gulp of his water and said with a sly smile, 'Do I need a brief?'

He saw the two men glance at each other. Then the tall one said, 'No, you don't need a brief, lad, not yet. This is an informal chat.'

69

Joe nodded, though he wasn't sure he understood. He was pleased with his question about the brief; he'd remembered that word from the things he'd watched on television – years ago, that seemed now. That would show them that he was no pushover. But he wished they'd get on and accuse him, if that was what they were here for. Get things over and done with.

Instead, the tall one, Lambert, said, 'How long have you been living here now, Joe?'

'Don't know exactly. Months, maybe.' He fixed his face into an inscrutable mask. That would show them that they weren't going to catch him out easily.

'Since Christmas, would you say?'

'Around then, yes.' It was after the new year when he came here, but he wouldn't tell them that.

'And where were you before that?'

'Can't remember. Another squat, I s'pose.'

'Had a job, have you, these last few months?'

He frowned. They must be trying to catch him for claiming the Social. But he didn't think he had, not while he was working. But the law was like a bloody great snake: they could have you for anything, if they put their minds to it. Best to be on the safe side. He said, 'No. Can't remember when I last worked.'

Lambert said, 'Be much better for you, Joe, if you were honest with us. About this and everything else.' He looked down at a sheet Joe hadn't noticed before, on his side of the shabby table. 'We made some enquiries about you before we came here, you see, Joe. Heard some good things, actually. That you'd kicked the drug habit. That you were in regular employment. Shelf-stacking at Sainsbury's, wasn't it?'

If they'd been able to find out about that, they probably knew everything else about him, were probably just playing cat and mouse with him in this dirty old kitchen. But you didn't live for months in squats without learning the code: you gave the police nothing. Nothing they could turn against you. Joe's lower lip came out in a sulky stubbornness. 'Casual work, that was. No guarantee of permanent employment, they said, when they took me on. Five pounds an hour. But I didn't claim the Social, not when I was stacking.'

'No, I don't believe you did. And you were doing well. Through the trial period and into a proper job. Mr Harding at Sainsbury's was quite pleased with you, when we spoke to him this morning. Hard-working and reliable, he said.'

Joe felt a stab of pride at that, although he was still determined not to trust them. Fancy old sourpuss Harding saying that about him! 'It wasn't hard, not really. Not after the first few days. And—'

'Until this week, that is. Mr Harding hasn't seen you since last Saturday, and he's had no word from you that you were sick. He didn't like that, Joe.'

Was it only last Saturday that he'd been at work? It seemed months ago, part of a better and vanished world. 'Couldn't help that, could I?'

'Couldn't you, Joe? Well no, perhaps you couldn't, not once you'd gone back on the heroin.'

Joe made to deny it, knew it was hopeless, let the thin arms he had lifted drop back hopelessly against his sides. Lambert's voice was suddenly harsh and angry. 'You're a fool, Joe, and you know it! You know what it takes to kick drugs, and you'd done it. Now you're throwing it all away!'

He wanted to deny it, and when he knew he couldn't, he wanted to beat his fists against that long, lined, unblinking face. The words were like nails in his splitting head. He shut his eyes and felt himself swaying as he gripped the sides of the chair beneath his thighs. Then, as a fit of trembling came again, he felt something warm and heavy about his shoulders. A coat. Not his coat. It must be the one that had been hanging on the back of the kitchen door. He was glad of its musty, enveloping warmth, but he must put it back as soon as they'd gone. Or leave it behind if they took him with them. People in squats didn't have many possessions, but they could cut up rough if they thought you were light-fingered with what few things they had.

They were speaking again, dragging him back to the world he had forgotten for a moment, as his brain hazed with the need for heroin. It was the burly one, the one who had helped him in, who had put the coat on his shoulders just now. Hook.

He said, 'You have a girlfriend, haven't you, Joe?'

'Had, you mean! Had a girlfriend!' The bitter correction was out before he thought. He saw them looking at each other, realized dully that he had given something away. In his grief and anger, he didn't care.

'Kate Wharton, wasn't it, Joe?' The sergeant's voice was slow, insistent, brooking of no argument from the fraying brain which needed its fix. Joe nodded.

'What happened to Kate, Joe?'

'She's dead.' He found the tears were flowing down the sides of his nose, down his cheeks, gathering on his chin. They accumulated there for a moment. Then he felt the first one drop on to the thin cotton of his T-shirt.

'How do you know that, Joe?'

He was dimly aware that there was a trap here. 'In the papers, isn't it? Found strangled, wasn't she?' He wondered if that was the right thing for him to say; he could no longer work out any tactics.

'That's right. I'm sorry, Joe. Got on well with Kate, did you?'

The tears ran still, surprising him. There was no sobbing, just moisture he could not control, running steadily from his eyes. 'Yes. She was my girl, Kate. We were going to be an item.'

'I see. Did Kate think that, too, Joe?'

Just like them to go questioning that; everyone used to ask him that, when Kate was still around. He said stubbornly, 'Yes. We were agreed. We were going to be an item.'

'But it never happened, did it?'

He shook his head dumbly, feeling the salt tears on his lips.

'Who killed her, Joe?'

They didn't know.

That message came leaping into his throbbing head. They didn't know what had happened between him and Kate, how it had all gone wrong. And he must keep it that way. He remembered the tale they had told him when he was taking the cure, about the millions of brain cells you lost when you were an addict. His head felt as though it hadn't many brain cells left within it at this moment, but he tried to muster them into a fierce concentration on that fact: they didn't know. They couldn't arrest him without evidence, and he wasn't going to give them any now. Not him. Not Joe Ashton.

The tears had stopped, as suddenly and unexpectedly as they had arrived.

He said, 'I don't know who killed Kate.' It came out slowly, with each monosyllable an immense effort.

There was a pause, and he knew they were studying him, but he didn't look up. Then the tall one, Lambert, started the questioning again. 'When did you last see Kate, Joe?'

He was careful now. They weren't going to catch him, for all that they had been kinder to him than pigs should have been. Perhaps that was all a trick. 'Last Friday night. After I'd finished at Sainsbury's.'

'And did she seem upset about anything?'

73

Still he concentrated, and still the words came to him when he needed them. 'No. She seemed just the same as she usually was. We – we had a laugh together.'

'And what was that about, Joe? What made the two of you laugh?'

He'd gone too far there. Given them something to fasten on, when he should have kept them guessing. 'I can't remember now. Nothing important.'

'And then the laughter stopped, and you had a bit of a row, I expect. Serious quarrel, was it, Joe?'

He didn't know how the switch to the quarrel had come, wondered what he'd done to let them get into that. He forced himself to think, to search for the right response. He mustn't look rattled. 'No, nothing serious. I'd have remembered what it was about, if it'd been serious.'

'Who killed Kate, Joe?'

It came as suddenly as a stone shattering a window. But Joe wasn't thrown by it. He kept his eyes closed, focusing all his failing resources on finding the right answer, on not making a mistake now, when he sensed it was nearly over. 'I don't know, do I? I'd tell you if I did, wouldn't I?'

'Would you, Joe? Do you know of any enemies Kate had, Joe? Think carefully now.'

Apart from me, they mean. Apart from me, after that awful quarrel. Why didn't you give way, Kate? Why did you make me fight? 'No. No enemies. None that would kill her, anyway.'

He was swaying now, holding hard to the seat of the chair at each side of his slender thighs, feeling he might fall on to the floor if he did not do that. The silence stretched, and he opened his eyes. They were both looking hard into his face.

Lambert said, 'We'll need to talk again, when you're in better shape. Before we go, you're sure you can't think of anyone who might have killed Kate?'

He shook his head, unable to speak now, frightened that his tongue would betray him if he did. He wanted only to lie on the mattress against the torn wallpaper of the wall upstairs, to curl up tight in the foetal position which might let him forget.

Hook turned when they reached the door, came back and spoke quietly but urgently into his ear. 'Don't give up what you've achieved, lad. Don't go back on the heroin, not now. Whatever else you might have done.'

Joe thought for a moment he was going to start the questions again, He nodded, without reopening his eyes. Hook said, 'Go and see Father Gillespie at St Anne's House. He's a good man. He'll help you, without asking questions. Get yourself round there this morning, in time for the meal at one. You need food, Joe. You're not hooked again yet, but you need help.'

Joe wanted only to be alone, wanted only to be rid of this unexpectedly kindly man. 'I will. I'll go there today,' he gasped. He struggled upright, reeled to the door, clutched the rickety handrail as he climbed the rotting stairs. When he reached the top and turned with a sigh, he found Hook still watching him from the kitchen door.

He leaned against the wall of the bedroom and watched the pigs through the cracked pane of the big sash window. The tall one folded himself stiffly into the car. Hook looked up at the white-faced watcher at the window and gave him a fleeting smile.

Joe watched them drive away. Then he fell face down on the stinking mattress, rolled on to his side, and drew his knees up against his chest.

Nine

Julie Wharton had made the bed during the morning. But she went up to the bedroom after the phone call, retrieved the pyjamas from under her nightdress, and shut them carefully in the drawer of the dressing table. She went into the bathroom and moved the razor and shaving cream from the washbasin to the cupboard beneath it. There was no reason why they should come up here, but she was taking no chances. You never knew where the police would poke their noses, if you excited their curiosity.

She looked at the time on the bedside radio. Two o'clock. She had half an hour yet before the time they had agreed. She went downstairs, set the small table in the kitchen with a single setting of cutlery and a single cup and saucer, and moved the shirts, socks and underpants from the clothes stand, where they had been airing. Then she vacuumed the floor in the living room, picked up Roy's picture from the sideboard and looked at it fondly for a moment. 'Got to keep you out of this if we can, haven't we, my love?' she said as she laid the silver frame in a drawer beneath the tablecloth she never used.

She was glad when they arrived. They were exactly on time, but she had been sitting in a chair watching the front gate for five minutes, getting uncharacteristically nervous. That lumpish Sergeant Hook had a tall man with a stoop behind him as he came up the path. This must be the Superintendent Lambert the paper had made into a local

76

hero when they reported that he had been put on to the Kate Wharton case. 'Top Cop Brought in to Probe Murder of Local Beauty,' their headline had said. He didn't look anything special, to her, but she'd better be on her guard.

Lambert's eyes were level with hers as she stood on the doorstep above him. They were grey, searching eyes which had no embarrassment in studying her. She took the two CID men into the living room and offered them tea, which they refused. As soon as they were sitting down, the superintendent said, 'I'm very sorry about Kate, Mrs Wharton.'

She allowed herself a little nod of acknowledgement. 'Thank you. I understand you discovered the body yourself.'

'To be strictly accurate, Sergeant Hook found her. But I was with him at the time.'

'Golf must be a good way for you to wind down. I don't play myself, but I understand Ross is a very good course.'

He wondered if he should really believe his ears. The bereaved mother, perfectly composed, discussing the way policemen relaxed and the quality of facilities in a game she did not play. It was too polite and artificial for him to believe she was doing anything other than diverting him from more important areas. But what areas? For all her assurance, she scarcely looked like a woman who would wrench a cord hard round the neck of her own daughter until she ceased to breathe. Bert Hook had already suggested one area to be explored, but he didn't want to start with that. He said, 'I'm sorry we had to put you through the ordeal of identification.'

'The law demands it. I was the obvious person, as her father is dead.'

'Indeed. But it is harrowing, nonetheless. There's one more formal ordeal for you, I'm afraid. There will be an inquest. You'll be called to give evidence of identification.'

'That won't be a problem.'

'The coroner will certainly be sympathetic. It's unlikely that you will be asked any other questions.'

She showed the first expression on that blank, polite face with its frame of neat dark hair: a flicker of irritation. 'You don't need to wrap me in cotton wool, Mr Lambert. I won't collapse in tears.'

'I'm glad to hear it. Because in that case, you won't mind helping us now, by answering a few more searching questions about Kate.'

She registered the harder tone in his voice, knew that the real business they had come here to conduct was about to start. 'Ask away.'

'What was your relationship with your daughter, Mrs Wharton?'

'She left home four years ago.' She watched the impassive Hook recording the fact in his round hand in the notebook he had produced.

Lambert said, with the air of a man whose patience is not inexhaustible, 'Mrs Wharton, our problem in a murder investigation is that it is the one crime in which we cannot interview the victim. We have to build up a picture, in this case of a dead girl, through the eyes of those who knew her when she was alive. We would expect a mother to be anxious to help us.'

'I'm answering your questions.'

'There are some cases where one can make a distinction between answering questions and being co-operative. I'd say that this is one of them, so far.'

She looked at him as if she was wondering whether to take offence. Then she said coolly, 'We weren't close, Kate and I. I haven't seen much of her, since she left home. That was her choice.'

'The leaving home, or the lack of contact afterwards?'
'Both.'

'You didn't visit her?'

'I didn't even know where she lived, after the first couple of years. She never came back here.'

'Didn't you care about that, Mrs Wharton?'

'I don't see that it's any of your business whether I did or not.'

'I can assure you that it is, now that Kate is a murder victim.'

'All right. We had a row. She walked out. Neither of us held out the olive branch, so we didn't meet up or make up. That may be sad, because death is so final, but those are the facts of the case.'

'Was Kate very close to you, in the years before she left?'

She pursed her lips and sat back a little in her armchair, as if considering the question for the first time. 'We weren't as close as many mothers and daughters are. You might have expected us to be, but that was the situation. Kate's father died eight years ago last week. She was very close to him and she was fourteen when he died. I had most of the troubles of adolescence to tackle on my own. We quarrelled quite a lot and there was no one else to share the load.'

Lambert nodded. He had taken two daughters of his own through adolescence, and he would have got it very wrong without Christine's help. 'Serious quarrels? I ask because many people come through such things and find themselves closer than ever. You sound as though that didn't happen for you.'

She looked into those penetrating grey eyes for a moment before she said, 'We were never very close, the two of us. I sometimes think I haven't the capacity for that sort of love.'

It should have sounded infinitely sad. It sounded flat and empty, but hardly regretful. It was issued as a statement of fact, rather than a plea for sympathy. Lambert could already see why Bert Hook had seen this woman as an enigma. He said, 'So you weren't close at the time of her death.'

'We were not even in touch with each other.'

There should have been a human tragedy here. But she presented it again as a bald summary of events, a reason why she could not be connected with this death. Lambert wondered for the first time whether this was indeed a tactic, a distancing of herself from a death victim so as to reduce suspicion. He said quietly, 'When did you last see Kate alive, Mrs Wharton?'

'It must have been three months or more before her death. And that was only a chance meeting. I ran into her in Gloucester when I was shopping.'

'And how did she seem then?'

'Unexpectedly prosperous. She was well dressed and cheerful. But we only spoke for a few minutes.'

'I'm afraid I have to tell you that she had been using drugs. She wasn't an addict, it seems, but she had certainly used drugs in the months before her death. Was there any evidence of this when you met her?'

'No, she seemed cheerful and optimistic. Would that be something to do with the drugs? I wouldn't know what the symptoms are.' She seemed happy to declare that; she did it with a small smile of satisfaction.

'You didn't notice any dilation of the eye pupils, any unnatural, febrile excitement?'

'No, nothing like that. But as I said, we spoke only briefly. Kate suggested we went for a coffee, but I hadn't the time.'

There should have been an infinite sadness in this last missed opportunity, but again she reported it merely as a piece of information, an explanation why she could offer little of interest about this dead daughter. Lambert said, 'Had she any enemies that you know of? Think carefully, please.'

'I don't need to. The answer's no. I've thought about it, since I heard about her death, of course I have. But I know so little about the way she has lived in these last years that I can't be of help.'

It was what he had expected, but the manner of its delivery again surprised him: she sounded content rather than regretful that she was unable to help them. 'Where were you last Sunday, Mrs Wharton?' he asked abruptly.

'Here, most of the day. I did some clearing up in the garden, ready for the bedding plants.'

'Were you alone?'

She considered the matter. He was quite sure that she knew what he was about, that he was asking whether she had a witness to her presence here at the time when her daughter died. 'The woman next door came in for a coffee in the morning. I met a friend for Sunday lunch at the Penny Farthing at Lea. I can give you her name.'

'And in the late afternoon and evening?'

'I was here. That's when Kate died, isn't it?' She was suddenly much more animated.

'We think so. Think about this again, please. Can you think of anyone who might have killed your daughter, whether on impulse or as a pre-planned crime?'

'No. I told you earlier, I was out of touch with Kate and even more out of touch with her circle.'

Again that calm dismissal, as if her only child had been no more than a distant acquaintance. Lambert felt his irritation rising further. 'How long have you been a widow, Mrs Wharton?'

'I thought I told you that. Eight years now.'

'Do you have a close male friend?'

'I don't see that that's any concern of yours.'

81

'Normally you'd be correct. But this is a murder inquiry, and we need to explore every avenue. Surely you want us to arrest the person who killed your daughter?'

She shrugged her trim shoulders. 'No. I know a few men, of course – I work with men in Cheltenham – but I have no close attachment.'

There was a pause. Hook looked up from his notebook and came in as Lambert had known he would. 'And yet you know some man well enough to do his washing, Mrs Wharton.'

She looked at him furiously – angry with him for his intervention, and with herself for underestimating the man she had thought so wooden. 'I don't know what you mean.'

Hook said mildly, 'When I collected you to identify the body of your daughter yesterday morning, there were male clothes on your washing line.'

'But you didn't come in.'

'Are you denying the fact?'

He must have looked down the row of back gardens from the end as he turned into the close. Crafty bugger! He sat there, looking a little overweight, like a bloke who'd eaten too much and was ready to fall asleep. And yet he had picked this up, in those two meetings where she thought she had given him nothing at all. She told herself not to panic, that she had always known it would come out about Roy, that there was really nothing lost here.

Yet she had been exposed in a lie: she was going to have to go back on what she had said. She forced a meaningless smile, said carefully, 'All right, there is a man. A boyfriend, if you like, though at forty-two I'm too old to deal in such terms. I have a lover, a serious lover.'

Lambert nodded. 'Whom you tried to conceal from us. Who might have gone unremarked, for a time at least, had it not been for Detective Sergeant Hook's alertness.'

'I wanted to keep my man out of this. That's natural enough, isn't it?'

'Perhaps. Unless he had any connection with this death, of course.'

'I can assure you he didn't.'

'Unfortunately we can't accept that assurance. Especially as you tried to conceal his very existence from us. We'll have his name, please.'

'His name is Roy Cook.'

'Is Mr Cook a married man?'

'Is that remotely relevant?'

'It is, yes. It would give you a reason for trying to conceal his identity from us. A reason which would be innocent, in terms of this murder.'

She flushed a little; Bert Hook thought that she looked slightly rattled, for the first time in three meetings. 'Roy is divorced. He had been separated for several years before that. Now that his divorce is through, we shall be getting married.'

'How long have you known him?'

She had not expected this detailed questioning – would have resisted answering, indeed, if she had followed her inclination. But she had got off on the wrong foot by denying Roy's very existence; if she sought to conceal the details of their relationship, they might question other, more hostile, sources. 'About seven years. We've been a couple for the last five.'

'Does Mr Cook live here?'

She would have liked to say yes, to claim they were married in all but name. But they were certain to question Roy now, and they wouldn't get that version from him. 'No. He has a small house of his own, on the other side of Gloucester. But he spends at least as many nights here as there, and does most of his washing here, as Sergeant Hook so observantly noted.'

83

Bert Hook ignored the acidity in her tone and took down the address. Lambert asked, 'Did Mr Cook know your daughter?'

She did a swift calculation. Kate, as they had pointed out so helpfully, wasn't here to give her side of the story, and she could brief Roy before they got to him; she'd be on the phone to him as soon as they left here. But there was a cool efficiency about these two. They weren't likely simply to accept what she and Roy said: they'd probably send someone in their team to question neighbours and other relatives. She couldn't afford to be caught out in another clumsy lie. She said, 'Roy did know Kate, yes, briefly.'

'How well did he know her?'

She hadn't been prepared for anything so direct. She thought of saying 'not in the biblical sense', but she knew this wasn't the time for flippancy. She said, 'Scarcely at all. As far as I remember, Kate walked out a few months after Roy and I had got serious.'

'And was her departure connected in any way with Mr Cook?'

This was important. She took her time, smiled at them to show how ridiculous the notion was. 'He didn't rape her, if that's what you mean! But Kate was eighteen at the time, and I suppose the arrival of any new man in what had been her father's bed might have had an effect. I don't think she liked it, but it wasn't personal: she hardly knew Roy.'

She was trying to be offhand, but Lambert fancied there was a little more here than she was prepared to concede. He made a mental note to press Cook on this one, in due course, though he was sure this cool woman would have her lover well briefed before they got to him. He stood up. 'We shall probably need to speak to you again, in due course, Mrs Wharton. In the meantime—'

Death on the Eleventh Hole

'Why is that? I assure you there is nothing more I can tell you.'

'We shall need to check out certain things about Kate. Certain impressions other people may have formed of her. We may need to discuss with you certain facts of which you are as yet ignorant. You say you know very little about the life your daughter led in the years before her death.'

She wondered how he managed to make those closing sentences sound so ominous. She watched them drive out of the close, then waited another two minutes before she rang Roy.

On a golden May evening, Lambert looked out of the window of the murder room in the car park of Ross-on-Wye Golf Club, decided enough was enough, and took Bert Hook out on to the golf course.

'Golf must be a good way for you to wind down,' the enigmatic Julie Wharton had said, and who was he to dispute this eminently sensible view from a member of the public they served? Bert Hook would have disputed it: within two holes, he felt he was being wound up rather than wound down.

Bert was quite pleased when his drive went straight down the middle of the first fairway. 'Try taking the club away more slowly, and make sure you complete your backswing,' said Lambert from his position at the edge of the tee, where he was assessing Hook carefully with his head slightly on one side. Bert did both – and topped his 6-iron second savagely through the green. Bert wasted a look of molten fury on his chief's retreating back, as Lambert walked away with his head shaking sadly over this incompetence.

Hook was winning the second hole, where his handicap gave him a shot advantage, from start to finish. He thought he was going to get through an entire hole without advice, but after he had trickled his winning putt into the hole, Lambert said, 'Your putting style isn't convincing, you know, but if you're happy with it, that's up to you, of course.'

'I'm happy with it!' said Bert through clenched teeth.

But he found that when he came to putt on the third hole, he was intensely conscious both of the style Lambert had thought unconvincing and of his mentor's intense scrutiny. He found it an immense effort to hit the ball at all. Eventually he sent it right of the hole with a sudden prod. He looked up to find Lambert wincing and looking up at the intense blue sky.

Bert couldn't go through this performance on every green. 'All right, John,' he conceded resignedly, 'what is it you think I'm getting wrong?'

Lambert leapt forward like a starving lion offered raw meat. He gave Hook what he called 'the orthodox reverse overlap putting grip'. He steered Bert's head over the ball and pushed the back of his knees forward with a 5-iron into what he called 'the orthodox semi-sitting posture'. He told Bert to rock his shoulders back and forth and keep his wrists steady. 'Now, try it again,' he said. 'I'm sure you'll find that much more comfortable.'

Bert struggled into position. Reminders about each of these instructions accompanied his every modification of a putting style which had seemed to him quite efficient. He kept his head rigid over the ball, not daring to move it, as he said from the corner of his mouth, 'I feel like an arthritic crab.'

'You'll soon find it feels entirely natural,' Lambert reassured him. 'There's no one behind us, so just try a six-foot putt before we move on.'

Bert did. The ball shot past the hole, six inches left of it. 'You putted that like an arthritic crab!' said Lambert sadly.

Hook received more instructions on his swing on the fourth and fifth. Perhaps because of his enthusiasm for imparting knowledge, Lambert's own game was increasingly erratic, a trend which Bert noticed but upon which he refrained from commenting. This saintly forbearance failed to stem the tidal wave of instruction. Bert looked at his watch. Past eight o'clock, and high tide at Bristol. The Severn Bore, that watery phenomenon so amazing to see, so impossible to resist, would be surging up the river ten miles to the east of them. The flow of Lambert's advice seemed to him like a similar irresistible force of nature.

The inevitable shattering of control in this patient man came on the sixth green. He caught a tutting from Lambert as he prepared to putt and whirled upon him like a furious gladiator. 'Look, John,' he said with ominous dignity, 'you may not have noticed, but I'm about to go three up, and we agreed there was only time for nine holes before dark. I suggest you get your finger out and give some attention to your own game! If you need any assistance in the way of advice, I'll give you whatever help I can!'

John Lambert's expression of shocked incredulity was wasted on his sergeant, who turned his back, holed his four-footer, and marched to the seventh tee. There was a heavy silence as he addressed his ball. His superintendent's hurt was not alleviated by the nagging thought at the back of his mind that Bert's outburst might have had a tiny morsel of justification.

But golf, as its literature never fails to remind us, is a strange game, perhaps the most unpredictable one of all. The last three holes were played in a strained silence, with each player trying desperately to concentrate on the matter in hand. Lambert's game improved. Hook's, perhaps because he was still a little aghast at the temerity of his uncharacteristic eruption, declined.

Lambert won the last three holes to halve the match.

They shook hands and smiled embarrassed smiles at each other in the twilight on the ninth green. Nothing needed to be said between colleagues who had never quarrelled in a decade of professional work together.

A half, in a contest that had seemed lost. Lambert drove home slowly but happily, his headlights catching the swooping of the occasional bat above the silent hedgerows. The boy in him sang his happiness. That had put bloody old Bert in his place.

Retirement wouldn't be too bad, really. He would be able to concentrate on raising his golf to still higher levels.

Ten

Industrial chainsaws are efficient but very noisy. They necessitate the wearing of earmuffs and goggles. It was Roy Cook's use of such a chainsaw that ensured that he saw the CID men before he heard them, and that they were very close to him before he was even aware of their presence.

He was cutting up a pine which the Forestry Commission had decreed must be felled for safety reasons, severing its trunk into manageable lengths for the lorry which would come in later in the week. He was completely absorbed in the task, as anyone handling dangerous equipment must be; concentration had become a way of life to him now. He listened to the muted sound of the saw through his earmuffs, knowing from the lower note of the whine when the saw was working hardest, watching for the moment of maximum danger when the blade leapt through the last section of the log as though it were butter.

He was conscious of the smell of sawn wood, of the rapidly rising pile of resinous sawdust at the edge of his vision. It took him a moment to realize that the two black objects he saw disappearing beneath a patina of yellow dust were human feet, inside what had a minute earlier been the shiny toe-caps of black shoes. He was startled, but his training prevented him from the physical twitch which might have manifested itself in a less experienced operator.

He completed the cut he had started in the bole of the

felled pine, watching the teeth of the saw cut steadily through the base of a trunk almost two feet in diameter, enjoying the symmetry of the neat cone of sawdust beneath his handiwork. Then he switched off the tool, slipped on the safety catch, and set it down, feeling the silence of the forest flooding slowly back into his ears as he removed the muffs and turned unhurriedly to confront the men who had interrupted his work.

There were two of them: the man whose shoes he had covered with sawdust, a rubicund country figure with the build and shoulders of a farmer, and a taller, leaner figure behind him, who seemed perfectly content to take in the scene and study the man at the centre of it. Only when the last echoes of the chainsaw had died away among the still tops of the trees did he take a pace forward, produce a warrant card, and say, 'I'm Detective Superintendent Lambert and this is Detective Sergeant Hook. I take it you are Royston Cook?'

'Roy Cook, yes. I didn't think you'd come here.'

'Saves time, for all of us. Do I gather you were expecting us to contact you?'

'Julie rang me last night. Told me you might want to speak to me. I won't be able to help you.'

'Perhaps not. But as you will know, we are pursuing a murder inquiry. So it's routine for us to speak to anyone who had a close association with the deceased.'

'I didn't have a close association.'

'You lived in the same house with her for some time.'

For a moment, Lambert thought he was going to deny it. But he must have thought of his conversation with Julie Wharton on the previous evening, when she had presumably passed on to him exactly what she had said about her daughter. For all he knew, the pair of them had spent the night together and planned his response, despite the man's immediate admission of the phone call.

Roy Cook eventually gave them a curt nod, acknowledging that he and the dead girl had spent time under the same roof. He was a big-shouldered man, taller than he looked at first sight because of his broad build, with thick black hair and bushy eyebrows, which were more prominent as he took off the goggles he had worn while crouching over the saw. The sleeves of his thick checked shirt were rolled up, revealing the power of immense forearms. He had the build of a rugby prop forward, the strength of the miners who had once thronged the Welsh valleys thirty miles to the south-west of here. Bert Hook, who still tended to assess men in cricketing terms, was reminded of the Fred Trueman whom he had watched taking his three hundredth test wicket when he was a boy. The thought also sprang unbidden into his mind that this man could have carried that slight corpse he had discovered four days ago as easily as a dead cat.

Cook now sat down on a newly exposed tree stump and waved his hand expansively at others a few yards away. 'We're not often short of a pew, in the forest,' he explained with a smile. For all the world as if he was welcoming them into his home, thought Lambert. And indeed, this place, with its forest quiet, its small patch of clear blue sky above the tops of the trees, its chatterings of distant birdsong, seemed a natural place for this powerful man, whose muscles were sheened in sweat, even in the moderate temperature of this spring day. The village smithy and its chestnut tree might be gone for ever, but its central blacksmith figure had found a place here, beneath other trees.

Lambert said, 'If you're straightforward and honest with us, we probably won't need to detain you for very long.'

Cook looked up unhurriedly at the patch of blue sky and the single bank of high white cloud that was crossing it. 'Forestry Commission won't bother about that,' he said with a thick, soft Gloucestershire burr. Like many big men, he spoke quietly, but his register was low – more basso profundo than Welsh tenor. 'Reckon they know I give good value, most of the time. They won't bother about me having a sit for ten minutes.'

Lambert smiled. 'I'll keep it as short as possible. How would you describe your relationship with Julie Wharton, Mr Cook?'

Roy shifted uncomfortably for a moment on the raw yellow of the tree-stump. Did they want to know about those frantic rollings in the darkness, when Julie became a different, uncontrolled woman, gasping and screaming, and releasing the primitive dark man from within himself that he had thought hidden now for ever? Julie hadn't prepared him for this.

He said stiffly, playing for time, waiting for his mind to offer him something acceptable, 'We ain't married, Julie and me. No reason why we shouldn't be, mind, but we likes it that way.'

A little different from the way Julie Wharton saw it: she had said they were planning to get married. 'You're serious about the relationship, though. You stay at her house, and she at yours.'

'Yes. Leastways, I stay at her house. Julie don't come to me, not often. I only have a small place.' He wouldn't tell them how he clung to his little house, his assertion of independence; how he resisted Julie's pressure to sell up and move in with her for good. That wasn't their business.

'But you lived with Mrs Wharton, for a time, a few years ago.'

'More or less lived with her, I suppose. I din't never give up me own place, though.' The Gloucestershire came out more strongly in his voice as he became less certain.

'The time when Kate Wharton was still living at home.'

'Would be then, yes, I s'pose.'

'In other words, you know it was then. So what was your relationship with Kate, Mr Cook?'

'Din't see much of the girl, did I? Were the mother I were interested in, not the daughter.' A lustful grin appeared and just as quickly disappeared, as if he had realized this was not the context for it.

'I see. Kate would be what age, then? About seventeen or eighteen?'

''Bout that, yes.'

Roy Cook was more intelligent than the shambling oaf he presented as he squirmed now on his temporary seat. But words were not his strong point, and this was an area where he knew he had to be careful. Julie hadn't let him down, wouldn't let him down in this. They'd discussed it, agreed the offhand, detached way he must describe him and Kate. But as a man who didn't trust words, who in a crisis was used to using strong arms and fists, he wasn't confident about how to hold people off.

It was Hook who now said quietly, 'Pretty girl, was she, Kate? She was very pretty when she died. I expect she was turning a few heads when she was seventeen or eighteen.' He looked steadily into Cook's deep-set brown eyes, until his bull-like subject's gaze dropped to the bits of shattered bark around their feet.

'Right enough her was a pretty young thing then, was Kate. But too young for me. Her mother were the right one for me.' He was unhappy with this, fearing that his voice, so unused these days to answering questions, to conducting a serious dialogue, would let him down. And in a way it did: he sounded as if he were trying to convince himself, as if he were obstinately repeating a line he had worked out before they came here. Perhaps he was aware he sounded unconvincing, for he now added unnecessarily, 'Her was a real woman, was Julie Wharton.

Pretty; good figure; tits every man around wanted to get his hands on.'

He looked at them, wanting to convince them, man to men. But it was an appeal which came straight from the public bar, suitable for men who had supped pints of beer or cider and were ready to get maudlin and lascivious together. Lambert looked at him without smiling. 'Why did Kate Wharton leave her mother and her home, Mr Cook?'

He tried to ease his big shoulders into a shrug, but could not co-ordinate the unaccustomed movement. 'Not on account of me. I never touched her!'

He was not a convincing liar, though he had had much practice in the past. His denial was too vigorous, and he sat upright, challenging them to refute it. Lambert said quietly, 'Neither of us suggested that you did, Mr Cook. It's interesting that you should rush to deny it, though. But you haven't answered my question. Why do you think Kate Wharton left home?'

'I dunno, do I? Best ask Julie why she went.'

'I'm asking you, Mr Cook. You were living in the house with the girl. You must have an opinion about why she left.'

He resisted the temptation to shout at them, to tell them to piss off and stop bothering him. That was never any good, with the police. He tried to think what Julie would say. They should have discussed this. 'I dunno why she left. She had other fish to fry, I expect. You should ask her.' He realized the impossibility of that, and said with a slow, embarrassed smile, 'But you can't, can you? Well, I can't help you. Her were a strange girl, were Kate. You'd best ask Julie about her: I could never work her out, myself.' He shook his head regretfully, as if recalling some eccentricity he would not reveal.

'We've asked Mrs Wharton about her daughter. We got

very little information from her. Why do you think that
would be?'

Roy Cook stroked his chin thoughtfully for a moment.
He was glad to have the focus removed from him and his
own feelings about Kate. But he must be careful not to
let Julie down; she had done well for him, and he must
look after her now. He said cautiously, 'They weren't
close, Julie Wharton and her Kate. Not for a mother and
a daughter.'

'And why would that be, do you think?'

'Don't know. Better ask Julie.'

'We did, without receiving any satisfactory account of
their relationship. That's why I'm asking you. Sometimes
the onlooker sees more of the game.'

Roy Cook hadn't heard that expression before. He looked
puzzled for a moment, then nodded his understanding. 'I
could never work the two of them out. I think Julie had
been very close to her dad, who was dead before I knew
her. I didn't want to seem to be taking his place, so I kept
out of it as much as I could.'

Lambert nodded. It was a convincing enough explanation of a difficult situation for the new man in Julie
Wharton's life. But it didn't take them much further into
this puzzling limbo of a relationship between mother and
daughter. And each time he successfully kept them at
arm's length, Roy Cook seemed to give off a tiny whiff
of satisfaction, as if he had scored a small point in a
difficult game. Hoping to catch the man off his guard,
Lambert deserted the formal language of interrogation and
said abruptly, 'Kate was a pretty girl. Did you try it on with
her yourself?'

Cook was flushed and angry as he looked up into the
clear grey eyes and the lined, watchful face. 'No, course
I didn't. 'Er wouldn't have looked at me, would 'er?'

'I don't know whether she would or not, Mr Cook, and

that isn't what I asked. I asked whether you tried it on with her, not whether you were successful.'

'No, I didn't. And you ain't got no right to go asking me 'bout such things.'

Lambert shrugged. 'I'm trying to find out all I can about a murder victim who isn't able to tell me these things herself. I'm puzzled about why she suddenly left home at eighteen. This is one possible reason. It's not the only one.'

'And it's not the right one, either. I'm telling you that.'

Cook's fists clenched and unclenched at his sides as he spoke, and Lambert could feel the physical strain of his self-control coming across the short space between them in that quiet place. He himself sat perfectly still, his only concern being to assess whether the man was telling the truth or not. The sound of a cuckoo came clear and mocking through the still air above the woodland, as if in derision of their efforts. He tried to knock his man off balance with another sudden switch. 'So who do you think killed Kate Wharton, Mr Cook?'

Cook's relief was palpable, but he did not rush into a sudden reply. Like many men who earned their living by hard physical labour, he was clearly uncomfortable with words. But Lambert was reminded again that it was easy to underestimate the intelligence of such men. This one took his time, relishing the switch of questioning away from himself, but weighing his words carefully before he spoke them. 'I wouldn't know that, would I? I ain't been in touch, not since she left home.' He looked the superintendent steadily in the eye, challenging him to deny the truth of the statement.

'So you don't know anything about the life Kate had been leading in the months before her death?'

'No. I couldn't, could I, being as 'ow I 'aven't seen 'er?'

'So you don't even know how she was earning a living?'

Again the clenching and unclenching of his fists before he said breathily, 'Look, how she behaved was nothing to do with me, see?'

'No, I don't see, which is why I had to ask the question. But I'm trying to see. Perhaps I shall know a little more when I've seen her flatmate.'

Lambert thought he caught a flash of fear in those deep-set brown eyes, but it might have been merely anger. Cook said with heavy control, 'I told you, I wasn't in touch. Neither was Julie. If the mother wasn't seeing her own daughter, it's hardly likely I was going to interfere, was it? As far as I was concerned, Kate was well out of my life, and it could stay that way.'

'And you've no idea who might have killed her?'

He looked for a moment as if he might say something, might perhaps venture some comment about the life she had led, the life about which he claimed to know nothing. Then he said formally, 'No, I haven't. I hope you find him though. Murderers shouldn't get away with it, or nobody would be safe.'

He sounded his aitches carefully in this, making it sound like the bland, prepared statement of a conventional virtuous attitude. Lambert stood up. 'If you think of even the smallest item that might be of use to us, it's your duty to get in touch immediately. We shall probably need to speak to you again in due course.'

If the last phrase had the ring of a threat, so be it. He was convinced that there was more to be had yet from this bear of a man, though he was not sure yet whether he was deliberately concealing information.

Roy Cook stood motionless and watched the pair walk a hundred yards away from him, until the track curved between tall oaks and they disappeared from his view. They were almost back at the car, half a mile away, when they heard the renewal of the raucous whine of the chainsaw and saw the birds wheeling in fright above their heads.

Later that Friday morning, Richard Ellacott popped his head round the door of the Secretary's office at Oldford Golf Club to see if there was any news. He liked to be apprised of any developments before the club became busy at the weekend when its working members arrived.

The Secretary told him there was nothing of note. The elderly member who was dying was holding on in the hospice, so there had been no need to fly the flag at half-mast. One of their youngsters had been selected for the Gloucestershire Colts team. Richard made a note of his name so that he could congratulate him in due course. He was on his way out of the office when the Secretary said, 'There are a couple of policemen in the lounge.'

Richard stopped with his hand on the door, trying to keep his voice even as he said, 'What do they want? Nothing wrong with our drinks licence, is there?'

'No, nothing like that. Just routine, they said. Apparently the police are visiting all golf clubs, in connection with this murdered girl at Ross. It's because she was found on the golf course there. They think other golfers might know someone who would have known the place to dump a corpse.'

Richard could hear the blood pulsing in his temples. He was surprised how calm his voice sounded as he said, 'They haven't got anyone lined up for it, then. They must be desperate, to be casting the net as wide as this.'

'I expect they are,' said the Secretary, transferring his attention ostentatiously back to the papers on his desk. He was tired of people popping their heads round the door to ask him about the police presence, anxious only to tidy up everything he could before the weekend.

Ellacott went into the spacious lounge of the club, which

at eleven o'clock on a Friday morning was deserted, apart from an elderly lady member who was talking earnestly to two young uniformed constables at the far end of the big room. She caught sight of Richard and said, 'Ah! Here's our Captain. I've no doubt he can tell you more about the golfing habits of the male membership than I can. I only came in to do the flowers!'

Richard beamed jovially, at the steward raising the shutters of the bar, at the lady who had introduced him, at the policemen, at the large, empty room. There was no end to his bonhomie, his wholesome good cheer, his air of happy innocence. 'Is there anything I can do to help?' he asked them cordially. 'Richard Ellacott at your service.'

Even the older of the policemen did not look more than twenty-one to Richard: His buttons shone bright on the carefully pressed navy uniform as he looked up and motioned the newcomer to sit down opposite them. He had plentiful, very glossy black hair, a smooth complexion, and clear eyes that must make women turn weak at the knees, thought Richard. Youth was very unfair.

The PC said, clearly repeating a formula he had worked out for this and other golf clubs, 'It's just routine, really. This girl Kate Wharton was found on a golf course. She'd been dumped in a ditch there, probably by someone who had spotted the place before as a useful spot to hide a body. We're asking people in golf clubs if they know of any person who might have been likely to commit such a crime and dump a body like this.'

By the end of his explanation, he was sounding weary of its repetition, as if he was going through a tedious exercise which he expected to produce a nil return. His defeatism gave Richard confidence. He said, 'You're casting a wide net, aren't you? There must be at least fifteen courses within easy range of Ross. With an average of, let's say, six hundred members. That's nine thousand people, for a start.' Richard was proud of his easy grasp of figures.

The constable gave him a bleak smile. 'That's true, sir.' He wished the superintendent who had set them off on this wild goose chase could hear the sensible calculations of this old buffer. He might look like a pompous twit, with his grey moustache and florid face, his old-fashioned sweater with the diamond pattern and the plus twos people wore for this poncey game, but he was talking sense.

But his colleague, PC Warburton, had aspirations. He nursed a desire he could not reveal to his uniformed companion for a transfer to CID. So he explained importantly, 'We obviously can't question nine thousand people. But in a murder hunt, we do have to spread the net wide, when there isn't an arrest within a few days. Information comes from the most unlikely places, sometimes. It's at least possible – we wouldn't say probable at this stage – that this killing has a golfing connection. And if we talk to people like you, who have an overview of their members, it's just possible that we might turn up that connection. I wouldn't put it any more strongly than that.'

Richard Ellacott tried not to smile at this assumption of gravitas by such a fresh-faced young constable. 'I see,' he said solemnly. 'Well, I'll give some thought to the matter. But I have to say that at present I can't think of any member who would fit the kind of profile you're suggesting. If we had any young rapists in the club with a bent for violence, I like to think we should have got rid of them long ago!' He laughed heartily at this sally.

PC Warburton did not laugh. He said gravely, 'Our killer may not be young, Mr Ellacott. May not even be a man, in fact, though that seems the likeliest possibility. And Ms Wharton was not raped.'

Richard was nettled by this correction from his young mentor. 'I see. So what exactly would you like from me?'

'Have you members who would know the spot on the Ross-on-Wye course where the body was concealed?'

Richard kept calm, took a moment or two to compose himself before he said, 'I imagine most of our members would have played at Ross at some time. There are matches between clubs, people have friends in the area who are members at Ross, we sometimes—'

'Would you yourself know the Ross course, for instance?'

This was becoming too personal for comfort. Richard said, 'Yes, of course I do. In common with hundreds of other people, in this club alone, as I pointed out earlier.'

'And you'd know the ditch on the eleventh hole at Ross where the body of Kate Wharton was found?'

Richard wondered if the blood which was drumming in his temples showed in his face. 'No, I don't recall the course in that much detail. I can't even picture the eleventh at Ross, and I certainly can't remember a ditch there.'

PC Warburton was not even looking at him. It was the reply he had expected, couched in words very similar to what he had now heard a dozen times. The fact that he stopped listening before the response was even concluded meant that he was not suitable for CID work, but he had no inkling of that.

'If,' he said, 'you think of anyone who might know the Ross course well, who might have had a connection with Ms Wharton when she was alive, please let us know. Any information will be treated in the strictest confidence, and the co-operation of people like you will be much appreciated, Mr Ellacott.'

It was a dismissal. Richard tried to be amused rather than piqued: he didn't think he had ever been dismissed by someone forty years younger than him before. He took the *Daily Telegraph* over to the other end of the big room and sat in a low armchair, pretending to be immersed in its contents.

He was right about the attractions of the young uni-formed policemen. Four middle-aged ladies who had come in for lunch swarmed around them, insisting they were fed, flirting outrageously, massaging the young male egos with their light female banter. They even tried hard to help them with their enquiries into the Kate Wharton murder. But they were not able to produce anything helpful while Richard was listening.

He couldn't eavesdrop for ever. Eventually he laid down his newspaper, waved a cheery farewell to the ladies who had neglected him today, assured the policemen that he would be in touch if he turned up anything of interest to them among his members, and left the club.

Three miles from the Oldford club, Richard Ellacott drove into a lay-by and sat very still for a few moments, unconscious of the birdsong and the bright spring day around him. The police didn't seem to be making much progress. The fact that they were going round golf clubs might even be helpful, in the end. Because he hadn't revealed the one vital fact that could undo him.

Eleven

M atthew Street, Gloucester, had been a good address, once. In the years after the house had been built, two thirds of the way through Victoria's long reign, coaches had dropped off important visitors here, and upper-class ladies had held their weekly 'at homes' for other females of their class. Even with the noisy advent of the horseless carriage in the early years of the twentieth century, the street had maintained its status throughout the short Edwardian era, when trade had dared to mingle with breeding in this gracious road.

The slow decline of the street and the area had begun like so many other declines after the first great world war of 1914–1918. The degeneration had accelerated after the even more wide-ranging cataclysm of 1939–1945, and once the unimaginable crimes of Fred and Rosemary West had been discovered a few streets away, there was no hope of Matthew Street being ever again a fashionable address.

Lambert and Hook parked the car and looked up at number fourteen for a moment before they went to the door. It was no better and no worse than the other high, three-storeyed houses in the Victorian street. Like most of them, it had lost its front garden, which a century earlier had twinkled with geraniums and lobelia, to a carpet of grey concrete, so that the ubiquitous motor cars of the tenants could be partially accommodated.

For these big houses had all now been divided into

smaller units. Cars in varying states of repair littered both the road and the house frontages, even early in the afternoon. Lambert and Hook walked past a battered Sierra and the steps which led down to a basement apartment and mounted the stone steps to what had once been a handsome blue front door. It was solid enough still, but scratched and in need of a coat of paint. Hook pressed the button at the side of the door which read 'Boyd' and the door was opened a moment later by a girl in clean blue jeans and a black shirt which was tight enough to outline small, neat breasts beneath the patch pockets.

The girl was in her early twenties, carefully made up for their visit. She hesitated a moment, waved aside their warrants, and said nervously, 'Yes, I'm Tracey Boyd. You'd better come up to the flat. I told you when you rang, we can talk there.'

Most of the rooms in this once gracious house had been divided, so that they had lost their proportions and the high Victorian ceilings seemed further away than ever. Tracey Boyd sat her visitors down in two battered armchairs and seated herself rather primly with her knees together on a sofa with a loose cover. 'You rent these places furnished,' she said, as if she felt a need to explain the drab décor. 'You don't have the chance to make much of an impact.'

They smiled at her, looking up the walls which needed a coat of emulsion paint to the dusty cornice that was almost invisible, high above the single light in the middle of the room. Hook said diplomatically, 'You've got the place very tidy.'

She sniffed. 'Your Scene of Crime team did that. Went through everything in the flat.'

Lambert smiled. 'We couldn't help that. It's routine to go through the home of a murder victim, as you probably realize. I understand you shared this flat with Kate Wharton.'

'Yes. We had a bedroom each, and shared the rest.'

The separate bedrooms were very necessary when they brought men back to the flat, no doubt. 'Why didn't you report Kate missing, when she didn't come back here on Sunday?'

It was a direct attack, with no preamble, and her pale face flinched a little in the face of it. 'I – I didn't realize at first that she wasn't here. We did our own things, gave each other our own space.' She brushed a strand of fair hair away from her left eye and looked at him defiantly.

'But you shared this place: you didn't have separate apartments.'

'We had separate bedrooms.'

'But you just told us that you shared this room, the kitchen and the bathroom. You'd know whether someone was in the place, whether you were close friends or not.'

'I didn't say we weren't close friends. I said we gave each other our own space.'

Lambert's voice hardened. 'You knew she wasn't coming back. You advertised for a replacement partner for the flat.'

The pale face flushed beneath the lank blonde hair. 'That was only yesterday.'

'Tuesday morning, the shopkeeper told our constable the advert was placed. He puts the date on the back of the postcard.'

'Bloody pigs! They've nothing better to do than persecute girls like me.'

'There's been a murder, Tracey. It's normal for uniformed police to check out the area where the deceased lived. When a young policeman is looking for accommodation himself, he's more likely to pick up an advert like yours; in this case, it carried a telephone number which he'd been given as part of the briefing for a murder hunt.'

'Bloody nosy young pig! I was only trying to get

someone to share the rent, before old Ma Eastham comes on to me for all of it on my own!'

'So you knew Kate hadn't come back. But you chose not to report it. It was left to Mrs Eastham to come and tell us that she had a tenant missing, on Tuesday. You must have known about it before she did.'

'She's a nosy old cow, Liz Eastham. Greedy for her rent, too. That's the only reason she came in to tell you.'

'We're not discussing why Mrs Eastham came to report Kate Wharton as missing. We're discussing why you didn't.'

'I didn't know why Kate hadn't come back, did I? There could have been all kinds of reasons.'

She was ignoring the point he had just made about her advert in the corner shop. She wasn't a convincing liar, this one. Maybe she would have been, to people of her own age, but not to experienced policemen. Lambert looked steadily into her glistening blue eyes until they could hold his stare no longer and dropped to the bright white trainers on her feet. He said quietly, 'How much money did you take from her room, Tracey?'

The young face which had been deliberately so blank when they came into the room was suddenly full of fear as well as resentment and he knew that he had struck home. 'I never . . . Well someone else would have had it, if it wasn't me. Old Ma Eastham, probably, saying she was owed it for her rent. And who's to say Kate didn't owe me money? She'd have wanted me to have it, anyway, would Kate. We were mates, weren't we?'

'How much, Tracey?'

'Two hundred quid. How'd you know, anyway?'

'I didn't. It was a reasonable deduction, that's all. There were only a couple of pounds on the body, and she hadn't paid anything into her bank account for a week. There should have been cash in her room somewhere, but the Scene of Crime team didn't find any.'

'You can have it back, I haven't spent it. It's almost a relief, if you want to know. I'd never have stolen from Kate, but I thought that old cow Eastham would claim it if I didn't.' Her pale face was flushed with the excitement and embarrassment of being discovered, and there was the relief that came with confession in it now. Lambert wanted to tell her that the money was irrelevant, that all he was interested in was who killed the girl who had shared this flat with her. Instead he said, 'Is that why you didn't come forward to report Kate Wharton missing? Because you had taken that money?'

'Yes. I'd have given it back to her, though, if she'd turned up. I'd never have stolen from Kate.'

'From your friend, no. You said that before.' He allowed a note of weary cynicism into his voice. 'Kate earned her money in the same way as you, didn't she, Tracey? On the game.'

'I don't know why you should say that. Can't you ever—?'

'Convictions for soliciting, last year, the pair of you, hadn't you?'

She looked for a minute as though she would deny it, would try to brazen it out. Then she said sulkily, 'Never give us a chance, do you? Couldn't pay for this place and save up for a place of our own, could we? Not in any other way. If men didn't bloody want it all the time, we couldn't sell it, could we? Bad enough having to make a living that way, without the bloody pigs trying to—'

'It's the law, Tracey, and as long as it remains the law, we'll have to enforce it. We all know that, so save us the persecuted toms argument. Right now, it doesn't interest me.' He leaned forward and spoke earnestly into the old-young, experienced face. 'But the way Kate Wharton earned her living does. And if blow jobs and golden rain and a dozen other sexual tricks got her money from men, I've got to be interested! Because every one of those punters is a possible killer, at this moment.'

'She only did straight sex, Kate. No extras. We used to tease her about that, about the money she was passing up.'

'She made a lot of money. We've seen her bank accounts.'

'You can do, if you're young and pretty. Men will do anything for young meat.' Her revulsion for the trade which supported her burst out in the contempt of the phrase. 'She'd have had to be less choosy, if she'd still been on the streets in her thirties. But she won't be, will she? Not now.' Tears brimmed suddenly in her bright blue, too-revealing eyes.

Lambert said quietly, 'You want to help us to find who killed your friend, don't you, Tracey?'

She nodded earnestly, oblivious of the tears which splashed silently on to her shirt with the movement. 'Course I do. She was a good friend, Kate. You make bloody sure you get the sod who killed her. Pity he can't swing for it!' Like many a petty criminal, she wanted the harshest penalties for people who committed more serious crime, and saw no anomaly in that.

'Reliable friend, was she?'

She looked at him suspiciously. 'I just said, didn't I?'

'You did. It's just that when people are shooting up with heroin, I wouldn't like to rely upon them too heavily, myself.' He dropped the bombshell in without even raising his voice.

They knew, then. They seemed to know everything, these two. Tracey Boyd said dully, 'I didn't do that, you know. We might have shared the rent and patrolled the same patch at times, but we weren't bloody twins!' She drew the sleeves of her shirt defiantly back, to reveal the smooth, unblemished skin of her arms, devoid of any trace of puncture marks.

But Lambert's eyes never left her face. 'I see. So you wouldn't be dealing either, then.'

She looked at him quickly, then down again at her feet as she said, 'I don't know what the hell you're talking about!'

'Oh, I think you do, Tracey. We have evidence that Kate Wharton was dealing; we can even deduce when fairly accurately, from the evidence of her bank deposits. At the moment, I'm more interested in who might have been her supplier than in whether you are a user or a dealer.'

'I'm not. I told you, I'm not even a user. I've seen too much of what it can do to people.'

'I'm glad to hear it. But Kate dealt. We know that. We want to know where she was getting her supplies from.'

She shook her head bleakly. 'I don't know. I'd tell you if I did. But I've always steered clear of that business. It frightens me to death.'

'It may have condemned your friend to death. You're sure she didn't tell you anything about her suppliers?'

'No. I didn't want to know, and she didn't want to talk about it.' She looked up at them, suddenly appalled by the thought that drugs might have been the cause of her friend's death. The blue eyes widened as she said, 'She was frightened to death herself about it. That's why she was determined to give up dealing.'

'When did she tell you this?'

Tracey Boyd thought hard. 'Last week.'

'Can you remember the day?'

She thought for a moment, her forehead wrinkling attractively with the effort, like that of a child anxious to please.

'Wednesday. About seven o'clock in the evening. Before

she—' Before she went out picking up men, she had almost said. Her small white teeth pulled hard at her lower lip and she fought back the tears. 'It was the last time we really spoke to each other.'

Lambert leant forward, trying not to seem too eager. 'Try to remember exactly what she said, Tracey. It might be important.'

She shook her head. 'Only that she'd given it up. That she wouldn't be having anything more to do with drugs. She'd given up using them and now she was giving up the supply.'

So the decision was quite recent. That might have been what the argument with Malcolm Flynn in the pub near the docks had been about, two nights earlier. 'You're certain she didn't give you a name? I'm sure you realize that it isn't easy giving up on being a pusher. Once these people have got their hooks into you, they don't let go easily.'

'No. But Kate didn't mention any names. She knew I was determined not to get involved, that I was scared of anything connected with hard drugs. And by that time, she was pretty scared herself.'

'If you think of anything, any other detail connected with the drugs, get in touch with us immediately.'

'I won't remember anything else. She never talked to me about it and, I keep telling you, I didn't want to know.'

That much at least rang true. Lambert tried another tack with this nervous girl, who seemed to be torn between a distrust of the police and a desire to see her dead friend avenged. 'Tracey made a bank deposit of twelve hundred pounds a month ago. That is much larger than her normal regular deposits. Do you know where it came from?'

Tracey Boyd looked puzzled. 'No. She wouldn't have made that on the game. We don't make as much as you lot think, you know, not when we've paid our rent. Tracey tried to put two hundred quid a week away. She wanted to give up the game, as well as drugs, you know. Most of us do, but not too many of us make it.'

'So let's say she put her normal two hundred in for the week we're talking about. What about the other thousand?'

Tracey Boyd shook her head. 'Drugs?'

'Perhaps. But there is no sum as big as that at any other time. She put smaller sums in regularly – usually around two hundred quid, as you say. Could she have let money accumulate and then put it in?'

'Not Kate. She didn't like having cash around the place. She put it in the Cheltenham and Gloucester as soon as she could.'

'So she didn't tell you where this thousand had come from.'

Tracey Boyd's face was full of conjecture about the sum. But all she said was a sullen, 'No. I've no idea. She didn't tell me everything.' She sounded resentful, but whether of her friend's secrecy or the relentless prying of the CID was not clear. Then she added, as if it were a consolation to her, 'If it was anything to do with drugs, I'm glad she didn't tell me.'

Lambert tried another sudden switch. 'Kate Wharton had a boyfriend, didn't she, Tracey?'

She looked for a moment as if she would deny it; she had made obstructing the police into a habit over the years. Then she admitted, 'A smackhead. I warned her off him, but she kept seeing him. Thought she could pull him out of it, I suppose.'

She affected a world-weary contempt for her friend's naivety. The CID men shared it to a large extent: they had seen too many women confident they could reform worthless men, and mistaken in that confidence. 'Give us his name, please, Tracey.'

'Joe something. I don't know his other name. I only met

him once. And I told you, he was connected with drugs, so that was enough for me.'

'Do you think he killed Kate?'

This time she was really startled by the bluntness of the question. She recoiled from it physically, inching back a little on the sofa. 'He might have, I suppose, if she tried to get rid of him. According to what she said, he was very keen. And there's no knowing what they'll do, is there, smackheads?'

'Indeed there isn't. For what it's worth, we've seen the boy, and so far there's nothing to connect him with Kate's death.' Whether he was guilty or innocent, the last thing he wanted to set in motion was a witch-hunt for someone in Joe Ashton's condition. 'Do you know the names of any of Kate Wharton's regular clients?'

'No. It's part of the deal. We never ask for names. Most of them are married men. Or professional men. Or policemen.' She gave him a bitter smile.

It was the response he had expected. Most people who paid for sex did indeed want to remain anonymous, and where the prostitutes did know a name, they knew they risked danger if they did not keep it to themselves. Indiscretions would mean that at best they would lose trade; at worst they would have their faces cut so badly that they would no longer be able to attract customers.

Lambert said gently, 'This is a murder inquiry, Tracey. We're looking for a man who might have killed your friend Kate, not just cheated on his wife.'

'I know. But I don't know the names of any of her regulars. It was understood we didn't exchange things like that.' Her face was expressionless, her mouth set into a thin slit, and he knew he would get no more from her, in this meeting at least.

Hook shut his notebook and the two big men stood up. 'If you think of anything, including names, which might be useful in our enquiries, it is your duty to contact us immediately. We shall probably be in touch with you again, when we have gathered more information. Kate's money will have to be returned to her estate, I'm afraid. Sergeant Hook will give you a receipt for it.'

She went and produced the two hundred pounds with a rubber band round it from her handbag, and handed it over with relief rather than resentment. She went down the single flight of stairs to the wide front door with them, as if anxious to make sure they were really leaving the premises.

Tracey Boyd decided she needed to indulge herself after that ordeal. She would make an exception and drink in the afternoon. She poured herself a stiff gin, filled up the glass with tonic. Then she sat for a long time on the sofa, leaning back into its cushions, trying unsuccessfully to relax, thinking about what she had given and what she had learned from the CID men.

She decided eventually that she had a good idea where that mysterious thousand pounds of Kate's had come from.

Twelve

When Lambert walked into the murder room on Saturday morning, he knew immediately that DI Rushton had some interesting information for him. Chris was only in his early thirties, a young man still to John Lambert, and his face could not conceal his satisfaction in having turned up a piece of information which his chief did not possess.

'It's Roy Cook,' said Rushton crisply. 'He's got a record.'

'So why didn't we know this earlier?'

'Because he changed his name. Ten years ago, when he was thirty-two.'

Before he knew Julie Wharton then, if the pair's accounts of their association were to be trusted. 'So what had he done?'

'Beaten up a woman. Because she refused him sex.'

'He did time, then.'

'Two years. He said he'd been led on, that the woman had wanted it, and then got scared. The usual mitigation plea. He was out in fourteen months, with remission. He was working on a building site in London at the time of the conviction. He changed his name to Royston Cook when he came out and came back to his native heath – he was born in the Forest of Dean.'

'Any other form?'

Rushton shrugged. 'Drunk and disorderly. Causing an

affray. Both around twenty years ago. He was bound over to keep the peace – treated leniently as a young man, I suspect.'

'Anything else?'

'He was almost brought to court on a rape charge, a year before the assault that got him sent down. The police in Battersea had the case fully prepared, but the case collapsed when the woman refused to give evidence at the last minute.'

The usual story. Understandable that women could not face the public exposure and the public humiliation of hostile cross-examination by a defence counsel, but highly frustrating for the police and the Crown Prosecution who had put in the time to prepare a solid case.

It gave Roy Cook an interesting background. He was now involved in a murder case where the victim had fought desperately before her death, had retained traces of that conflict under her nails.

Bert Hook had been standing at Rushton's shoulder, reading the information as it came up in the file Rushton had allotted to Roy Cook on his computer. He looked up into his chief's intense face. 'Do we go and see him now?'

Lambert frowned. 'I'd rather arrive without giving him notice of our visit so he can prepare himself. It's Saturday, and my guess is that he's more likely to be at Julie Wharton's than at his own house. Let's try there.'

He was sitting in the driving seat of his old Vauxhall Senator before a panting Hook had even reached the passenger door.

Father Gillespie watched Joe Ashton with a troubled face. The boy was eating at last, but away from the others, at a small table on his own. He had refused the support of numbers, still looked abstracted and intense, as if his mind was elsewhere and he scarcely knew what his body was doing. But he was eating. He had already had a plate of cereals, and now the scrambled egg and toast was disappearing rapidly. He had looked like a lost soul when he had wandered into St Anne's House on the previous evening. Even after a night's rest, his cheeks were hollow and his eyes were sunk deep into their sockets.

Father Jason Gillespie made it a habit not to wonder what people had done, to offer shelter and support without asking questions. It was why people came to St Anne's, why he had been able to rescue people who had one stage further to fall to prison or to a painful and ignominious death. But Joe Ashton's appearance set him thinking about the visit here by that stiff, well-meaning policeman, DI Chris Rushton, and the questions he had asked about a dead girl. This boy had seemed to be one of his successes, well on the path to a normal life. Was he now guilty of the worst crime of all?

Joe Ashton had not taken heroin on the previous night. He wasn't an addict, not any more, and, for the first time since Kate had died, it was important to him to prove that to himself. That is why he had come to St Anne's House: he was aware that he needed support if he was to do without smack, to pick himself up from the trough. He had tossed restlessly far into the night, had fallen into a troubled but restorative sleep at around half past four, when the first notes of the dawn chorus were shrilling round the eaves of the old house.

There were eight others in St Anne's House that night. All of them were down at breakfast while Joe still lay face down and asleep on the thin mattress upstairs. It had taken Father Gillespie, shaking his shoulder and virtually ordering him to rise and eat, to get Joe down to the dining room. One or two of the others looked at him curiously when he went and sat on his own, but they were too full of their own problems, too apprehensive of a harsh, perhaps

even violent, rebuff, to approach the old-young, drawn face
in the corner of the room.

Because the others had almost finished when he arrived,
he was alone in the big room by the time he had eaten
his food and clutched his mug of hot tea in both hands,
wondering what to do about the bleak world around him.
Father Gillespie, who seemed over the years to have built
up a feeling for such things, arrived at this crucial moment.
He slid into the chair opposite Joe and said, 'So what
happens today, Joe?'

'I don't bloody know!' Joe spat. 'Come here to give me
a fucking bollocking, have you?' He didn't swear much
nowadays, was surprised to hear the words issuing from
his lips. Father Gillespie wore no cassock, but his calling
was a provocation to a man steeped in despair.

Jason Gillespie was unshockable. He had been through
far worse than this, had swallowed blasphemy and obscenity
for weeks on end with some of his guests, had sometimes
endured months of such treatment with only the bitter taste
of failure at the end of it. He said with a gentle smile, 'Better
out than in, stuff like that, Joe. But it doesn't take the day
away, and doesn't answer the question about what you're
going to do with it. And I'll give you a bollocking if I think
it's necessary. I've told you before: I'll help all I can, but
bear in mind that the kick in the pants might be part of the
therapy.'

Joe Ashton looked up into the lined, experienced face,
with its kind but challenging grey eyes. Jason Gillespie
was actually forty-four, but to twenty-two-year-old Joe he
seemed immensely old and immensely knowledgeable. Joe
felt an sudden, enormous consolation in that thought; it was
as if his desperate life and its decisions could be taken out
of his hands by this sage from a different world. He said,
'There's bugger-all I can do, is there, Father?'

'There's always something you can do, Joe. You can

pray, for a start, throw yourself on God's mercy and ask for His guidance.'

'As far as I'm concerned, God can go fuck Himself. He doesn't exist.'

'Be a bit difficult that, if He doesn't exist. You'll find He's still there, when you're ready for Him. In the meantime, you could get yourself off to Sainsbury's and ask for your job back.'

'Fat chance of that! I haven't been near the bloody place for a week!' It seemed so much longer than that, to him.

'Tell them about Kate dying. About how upset you've been since then. I'll ring them for you, if you like, prepare the way for you.'

Joe thought for a moment, looking at the scratched Formica of the table top. Those coppers who had come to see him in the squat had said that old sourpuss Harding at Sainsbury's had thought he was a good worker. He might just get his job back, if he went now. He was aware, without admitting it even to himself, that he needed the routine of work. 'I don't need bloody priests to speak for me,' he said roughly. 'I'll go down there myself, when I've had a wash.'

'That's good, Joe. And give yourself a good shave, with the electric razor up there, won't you? They like a good appearance, in food stores.' He was wondering whether he might make that preparatory phone call anyway, whether he could rely on the manager at Sainsbury's not to tell the returning black sheep that someone had spoken up for him. Joe didn't reject the advice about his appearance, so Father Gillespie said, 'It was rotten about Kate, Joe. Still is, I know. It won't bring her back, but the police will get whoever killed her, you know.'

Joe looked up sharply, and the priest saw panic flooding into his face. 'They will, won't they? I was sure they would, when they came to the squat.'

Jason Gillespie wasn't sure whether the note in the boy's voice was of satisfaction or of dull despair. 'Do you want to talk about Kate, Joe?' he asked. 'It might be a help, you know.'

'I can't, Father. You don't understand.'

'Maybe I might, though, if you talked about it.' This was not the confessional, where the boy would be asking for absolution for his sins, and the priest would be bound to secrecy. This boy had no religious belief, not at present. But the priest saw a troubled soul, and knew the benefits of release which sometimes came with talking. He said, 'You and Kate were good mates, weren't you?'

'She was on the game. Dropping her knickers to anyone, for a few silly quid.'

'I know that, Joe. There are worse things than that. You must have thought so, too, or you wouldn't have bothered with her.'

'Drugs, too.'

'I didn't know that. But you can kick the habit, as you know from your own experience.'

Joe shook his head. 'She'd given up that. She was never a smackhead, like me. She'd given up dealing, too.'

'That was good.'

'I wanted her to move away. Start afresh with me.' His voice had suddenly acquired a dreamy tone as he voiced the escapist vision Father Gillespie had heard so often before. He looked at the priest and said in a sudden burst of candour, 'We were going to get married. We'd have been all right, you know.'

'I'm sure you would, Joe. And if—'

'But we had a row. A terrible row.'

Jason Gillespie was suddenly not sure he wanted to hear the end of this. He said, 'I think you should get round to Sainsbury's as quickly as you can, really. And if they want someone to guarantee that you'll—'

'The most awful row you could imagine, Father. I wanted her to give up the game and come away with me right now. She said we needed just a bit more money. That if I gave her three months she'd have it. I couldn't face that. Kate being with other men, doing the sorts of things that—'

Suddenly his face was in his hands. Father Gillespie watched the slim shoulders heaving for a moment, then said, 'I can understand that. I don't think I could have lived with that, either.'

Joe Ashton's voice was muffled by his fingers: 'We had this awful row. She scratched me. I hit her.'

Jason Gillespie had a sudden, throat-constricting fear of what was coming next. He pulled the skinny young hands away from the anguished face. He heard himself saying, 'It's all over now, Joe. Best get yourself tidied up and over to Sainsbury's. I'm sure they'll want you back.'

Joe Ashton turned at the door. 'I'm sorry I swore, Father,' he mumbled as his last words before he disappeared.

Father Gillespie had forgotten all about the swearing.

They arrived at Julie Wharton's house without announcement, as Lambert had planned. But if she was surprised to see them at ten o'clock on a Saturday morning, she gave no sign of it.

The only difference in the sitting room from their last visit was a photograph of Roy Cook on the sideboard, which confirmed Lambert and Hook's view that it had been deliberately removed on their first visit to conceal the fact that she was so close to the man. And thus to keep Roy Cook out of the case: in view of what DI Rushton had just told them about the man's previous record with women, that was an interesting thought.

She asked them to sit down, then showed a hint of

underlying nervousness by asking the first question. 'Have there been any developments?' she said. It was a cool enquiry about a case which might have been quite distant from her, rather than an anguished request for news about the hunt for the killer of her dead daughter.

Lambert was irritated as he had been at their previous meeting by this seeming absence of emotion. He ignored her words and answered with a question of his own. 'Is Mr Cook here?'

'No.' She looked at the TV remote control, which was on the low table beside Bert Hook's armchair, where Roy had sat last night. Men always had to have the remote control, even when they put on the programmes you wanted. 'He was here overnight, but he's gone into work this morning. He said the overtime would be useful, and you have to take it whenever you get the chance with the Forestry Commission.'

Lambert nodded. 'I suppose you know he changed his name.'

If she was shaken, she did not show it. She paused for a couple of seconds, weighing her words before she said, 'I do know that, of course. And if you've discovered that, I suppose you also know about his record.'

'Yes. We know he went to prison. For assault upon a woman.'

'Yes. You don't know what the woman had done to him.'

'But the judge and the jury did, when he was given two years in prison.'

'You may say that. Perhaps you have a greater faith in British justice than I have.'

'Hardly. Any experienced policeman has seen dozens of people get away with crimes he knows they have committed. It's the price we pay for a fair system, they tell me. So you know about Roy Cook's time in gaol. Do you also know that on another occasion he was suspected of rape? That the charge was only dropped because the woman concerned refused to give evidence at the last minute?'

For the first time, she showed the anger he had been looking to provoke. 'Yes, I know about the rape accusation. As it happens, we don't have secrets from each other. What is this, character assassination?'

Lambert shrugged, as impassive now as she had been when she talked so coolly about her dead daughter. 'You might not have known. Most women would be anxious to hear the truth about a man they intended to marry. But I'm glad the man has been honest, in this case.'

'He came back here and made a new beginning. Got himself a job with the Forestry Commission, worked hard, held it down. Roy turned over a new leaf. That's what people are supposed to do when they've been in stir, isn't it?'

'Indeed it is, Mrs Wharton. And I'm glad he's been so frank with you. I'm sure you're a great help in keeping him to his new way of life.'

She looked at him suspiciously, her face flushed within the neat frame of short dark hair. She thought she had caught a note of irony, but there was no smile on the long, watchful face. 'We get on well, Roy and I. He makes no secret of the fact that he was a rough diamond when he was younger.'

Lambert thought that the things he had done made him a little more than that. But love in early middle age, whilst it may not have the blindness of youth, will yet turn a blind eye to things it wishes to ignore. 'So as far as you know, Mr Cook has had no trouble with women since he came back to this area?'

Julie Wharton had recovered her composure now. She could think clearly, and she realized they wouldn't be questioning her like this unless they had Roy in the frame for Kate's murder. Just like the police, to go for the man with the previous record! Take the easy way, whether or not it was the correct way. This was the moment when she must support her man.

She wished at this moment that Roy was here, sitting by her side, that he could hear the conviction she put into her voice as she said, 'Superintendent Lambert, Roy's learned his lesson; he's a changed man. He doesn't look at women, apart from me. You won't see him in court again.'

'I'm glad to hear it. We're always glad to hear of the reformed sinner, believe it or not.' This time he did smile. Then he cleared his throat and said, 'Why did he move out of this house four years ago?'

She was shocked by the suddenness of this, as he had intended she should be. She forced herself to think rather than reply in anger. She didn't know exactly what Roy had already conceded to them. She could make something up, but these two had caught her out in a lie last time they had been here, and lies only attracted attention to the very areas you wanted to conceal. She bought herself a little time by replying stiffly, 'I don't think this is any of your business.'

'Even if it has a bearing on your daughter's death?'

'It has no connection with that. But since you seem determined to ferret it out, Roy made a pass at Kate.' There, she had said it. If Roy had already let out this to them, they couldn't trip her up.

There was a heavy silence, during which she was conscious of both men studying her flushed face whilst she tried to look unconcerned. 'A serious pass, obviously, if you flung him out of your house for it,' Lambert commented.

Julie was glad to find she could think so clearly, in this crisis. Kate wasn't here to give her version of that awful day, and Roy was sure to play it down, if the police

123

confronted him with it. She would tell Roy exactly what she'd said, as soon as she got the chance – before these jackals got to him, certainly. She said calmly, 'Looking back at it, it was something and nothing. I overreacted.'

'That doesn't seem characteristic of you, if I may say so. Anyone who took someone who had beaten up and raped other women into her bed would hardly be likely to overreact.'

'Well, I did. Women in love do strange and illogical things, as you may know – or haven't either of you ever been in love?'

'So you flung him out for some minor assault on your daughter's virtue. Stole a kiss, did he?'

'Not much more than that.' She tried not to hear Kate's long, anguished scream, not to picture the scene when she herself had come back into the house on that day. 'Kate was a pretty young girl of eighteen with developing curves, who favoured short skirts. Roy is a red-blooded male. I should have seen that he would be tempted. It was something and nothing, really. Kate overreacted, and so did I.'

For the hundredth time since this death, Julie found herself asking forgiveness from the shade of her dead daughter. She had to say these things, to protect the man she loved.

Lambert's eyes had never left her face. 'I see. So on the strength of what you describe as a minor incident, you flung him out of your house.'

It was the second time he had used that phrase, as if he was determined to provoke her. She couldn't explain it by saying that this minor incident came from a man who had raped and assaulted different women before: she had played that down a few minutes earlier. She said, 'We wouldn't have got back together if it had been anything very serious, would we?'

Except, of course, that she could not do without the

feeling of Roy inside her, couldn't do without the violent, almost vicious, sex he had brought to her, the thing which brought her alive, made it impossible for her to think of him in some other woman's bed. But they wouldn't divine that, would they, these sluggish men, with their passions under tight control?

Lambert's continuous, unembarrassed study of her face made her feel that he saw everything, that he read her every thought, even though she knew that was impossible. 'Is that why Kate left home?' he asked.

They had come back to this again. She must pretend again that Kate meant nothing to her, as she had done from the start. 'No. It was about that time, but it was a variety of things. She wanted the freedom of being on her own, as young people do. It was nothing to do with Roy's forgetting himself for a moment.'

Forgive me, dead daughter, I have to do this. This is the man I love, God help me.

'I see. The timing was just a coincidence. Better make a note of that, Sergeant Hook.'

This time she was sure as she watched Hook's clear, round hand that Lambert was taunting her. But whatever they thought, she didn't see how they could get any other version of events, with Kate gone; Roy would certainly play it down as much as she had done.

They rose to go, and she relaxed. Then Lambert, using a favourite tactic of throwing in a key question when his subject thought the exchanges were over, said casually, 'Did Mr Cook see Kate again, after she'd left home?'

'No, of course he didn't. Once a young woman has made an absurd fuss over a playful gesture, you steer well clear, don't you?'

'I expect you do, if you've any sense, yes. Goodbye for the present, Mrs Wharton.'

Julie was glad she'd given Roy her mobile phone. She

was able to ring him as soon as the police car turned out of the close.

Sitting in the passenger seat of Lambert's old Vauxhall, Bert Hook put the hair carefully into a small plastic bag. This hair from Roy Cook's armchair would go to forensic, like the hair he had taken from Joe Ashton's mattress. You had to help the law along a little, at times. If there was no DNA match with the tissue samples taken from beneath the dead girl's fingernails, it might help to eliminate innocent men from the investigation. If there was, it would bring them back very swiftly to know the reason for the match.

Malcolm Flynn had no idea that he had been connected in police minds with the death of Kate Wharton.

He had not seen her again after their argument in the pub near Gloucester docks on the night of Monday 30th April, when she announced that she was no longer dealing in drugs and proposed to cut her associations with the trade. He had read the accounts of her death with interest, and had speculated privately about how that death had come about.

That was as far as he had allowed his curiosity to run. In his dark trade, you didn't speculate publicly about how the small people at the fringe of the industry might have met their ends.

On this Saturday night, twelve days after he had last seen Kate Wharton, he had more important work in hand. Two of his dealers were collecting their supplies. You didn't do this kind of thing around pubs: you might meet people there, might negotiate with individuals, but when you were carrying large quantities of illegal drugs, you needed quieter places, where you could more easily forecast the numbers and the types of people around.

This depot for wholesale building supplies was neither derelict nor disused, like some of the other places they used. But as a dropping zone for drugs, it had two big advantages. First, it was not in a cul de sac: dead ends allowed you to be trapped with no escape by the police, in the unlikely event of a tip-off. Malcolm could drive slowly past the deserted entrance to this building and, if he saw anything amiss, any vehicle which should not have been there, he could simply continue upon his way like an innocent citizen. Secondly, the fact that this yard was a busy centre of activity all week meant that it was not considered a likely rendezvous for more dubious dealings, whereas some of the derelict warehouses in industrial wastelands had been exciting the interest of the Drugs Squad of late. This place was quiet as the tomb on a Saturday night, but not thought of as deserted by the police and the public at large. He had used it at irregular intervals for almost a year now.

Malcolm turned his van slowly into the wide street between the high buildings. This was the time of high danger for him: if you were stopped with illegal narcotics with a street value of over a hundred thousand pounds in the back of your van, you were in trouble, whatever story you might come up with. The risk/return ratio was what had drawn him into this trade: you took what you saw as a small amount of risk in return for lucrative pickings. But these were the times when you took the risk. He would have every nerve attuned for the next fifteen minutes or so.

Everything was as he had expected. He stopped for a moment, inspecting the street ahead, checking his watch. Through the quiet air above the old city, he caught the sound of a church clock striking eleven. The hour when the pubs would be emptying; when the police would be occupied with noisy Saturday-night revellers and drunken brawls; the hour arranged for his drop. He eased the van gently forward.

The deserted street was inadequately lit, and the lamp nearest to the entrance to the building supplies centre was conveniently inoperative. The wide entrance to the yard, set back from the road to allow entry for the heavy lorries which moved in and out continually through the week, was almost in darkness.

He switched off the power and freewheeled the van the last few feet into this semi-circle of shadow. This moment with the handbrake on and the van at rest was always the worst, when you felt absolutely helpless and the seconds stretched like minutes.

The muffled knock on the side of the van came in less than a minute. It was a tiny rap, but it blared like the trumpet of doom in the ears of a man who had once been a God-fearing child. Malcolm, although he had been waiting for the sound, although he was in fact relieved by it, started like a guilty thing upon a fearful summons. He had read that, some time long ago; the phrase he thought he had forgotten came thudding into his mind as he struggled out of the driver's door.

The others were more frightened than he was, and that, in a curious, illogical way helped to calm him. He was the senior man here, the man who controlled their destinies: he had better show some composure, some grasp of the situation.

There was only one man there when he slid out from the driver's seat, but a second figure, then a third materialized from the shadows before he had opened the rear doors. They wore dark clothing, and hooded their faces like conspirators, but he checked each of the white faces in turn. Two males and a female. They were the ones he had expected. It was going according to plan, as he assured them at each meeting that it would.

The words exchanged were kept to a minimum. No one wanted to be kept at this point of exchange, the most dangerous one of all, for any longer than he or she could help. They conversed in hoarse, urgent whispers.

Ecstasy, cocaine, crack, heroin: the stable products of this dark industry. And the new 'date-rape' drug, Rohypnol, swift in its effects and undetectable a few hours later, was much in demand: each of the four wanted more than he could supply.

He had cleared almost everything from his van and the group was about to split up as silently as it had assembled when all hell was let loose.

The tall gates of the yard, which they had thought securely padlocked as usual for the weekend, swung suddenly open, and there was a single yell of 'Armed police! Stay exactly where you are and raise your hands!' followed by a confusion of other shouts as dark-clad cops swarmed like black bees from the offices which had seemed empty. The manic wail of sirens tore the quiet night apart, and two police vehicles arrived from each end of the street they had thought was safely deserted.

Malcolm Flynn, splayed like an obscene starfish over the warm bonnet of his van, felt hands running up the inside of his thighs and beneath his arms to make sure he carried no weapon. He turned when he was bidden, saw in the harsh white of the police headlamps the microphone which had been recording his whispered dealings, high on the gate above him.

The risk ratio did not seem so favourable now. Malcolm Flynn wondered as he sat between two impassive constables on the back seat of a police car how many years inside his easy pickings would cost him.

Thirteen

Tracey Boyd wasn't at her best on a Sunday morning. She'd had problems the previous night. Her first client had been a lawyer, who claimed that his feelings of guilt affected his performance. It had taken him a long time and a deal of tedious titillation with the removal of black underwear by Tracey before he could perform. When he did, it brought him relief rather than an ecstasy, and left him full of apologies she had not the time to hear.

When she had bundled the lawyer out and got back on to the streets, she had picked up a beery Irishman who refused to wear a condom. They were against his religion, he assured her repeatedly; presumably prostitutes were not. She had first insisted, then assisted, and finally endured. His eventual climax was so vigorous and so noisy that she feared old Ma Eastham would be certain to hear and demand an increase in her rent.

When it was all over, the Paddy claimed it had been like washing his feet with his socks on and demanded a refund. Fortunately, he had been too exhausted and too drunk to turn violent; indeed, he had become quite maudlin and claimed Tracey reminded him of his mother by the time she finally managed to turn him out on to the silent street.

She lay in bed until after half-past nine on the Sunday morning, watching the sun get stronger and higher behind the thin curtains, listening to Gloucester coming slowly alive around her. She had showered as she always did before going to bed, washing away the men and all she could of the evening. But she washed her hair when she rose on this Sunday morning, and dried it unhurriedly with her old electric drier as she read the front pages of the *People*. The royals had been at it again, apparently. Bonking away like rabbits, and Head of the Church of England. That always amused Tracey.

She spread her toast with the thick layer of lime marmalade that denoted relaxed luxury for her, and took it into the sitting room to savour it, while Radio One boomed in her ears from the hi-fi tower Kate Wharton had brought with her to the flat. She was curled up on the sofa in her dressing gown, still only halfway through her coffee, when the coppers arrived.

The same pair who had come here on Friday, the same watchful, distrustful air about them. Tracey decided she preferred even the coppers who occasionally arrested her to these two; those uniformed men had a cheery, impersonal banter with them, a sense of being involved in the same elaborate game which was set up by the law of a hypocritical land. Prostitution was a strange crime: it seemed to bring no real hostility from the police who had to enforce the law, and understanding rather than resentment from the women arrested.

Through the speaker at the door, she told the CID men to come up, then wondered if she had time at least to put on some make-up, and decided she had not. She felt vulnerable in her dressing gown, with pale shining face and her hair parted but still unbrushed after being washed. It seemed to her that it was more difficult to deceive these efficient, experienced men when she was in this state than when she was dressed and fully made up. Clothes and make-up were after all the tools of her trade, and Tracey Boyd felt at a disadvantage without them.

'Sorry to disturb you on a Sunday, Miss Boyd,' Lambert said briskly. 'More questions. Inevitable, really.'

'I don't see why. I told you all I could on Friday.'

'Our Scenes of Crime team found a few names in a diary they took from a drawer in Kate Wharton's dressing table. We'd like to check out whether they mean anything to you. Do you recognize this diary?'

She took the small leather-backed book from them. 'No. I've never seen it before. Not that I remember, anyway.'

It was a pathetic, touching link with the girl who had laughed and cried with her in this room. They had eaten boxes of chocolates together, drunk the odd bottle of cheap wine, watched weepy films on the television set in the corner. Now all that was left was this book with its blank pages and its occasional, puzzling note. She looked automatically for Sunday, 6th May, the day on which Kate had died. It was completely blank, of course, and its whiteness seemed to emphasize the awfulness of her death. The police, and particularly these two big coppers before her, must have looked eagerly for this page, and been even more disappointed than she was to find no assignation noted there, no clue as to whom Kate intended to meet on that last, fateful day.

Lambert said gently, 'The names are at the back of the book.'

There was a question mark at the top of the page, then three names in Kate's rather uneven hand. Tracey looked hard at the small page with this minimal information, not daring to look up at the men she knew were studying her every reaction. The name she knew was there, the first of the three; she did not know either of the others.

Tracey Boyd looked at them for a long time, pretending to be cudgelling her memory while in fact she composed herself to speak. She still did not trust herself to look at

Lambert when she eventually said, 'I'm sorry. None of these names means anything to me.'

Her voice sounded both confident and regretful in her own ears, and she was emboldened to look up into Lambert's watchful face. She was half delighted and half appalled by her ability to deceive.

Lambert got home early for Sunday lunch. His daughter Caroline and son-in-law, a BT manager he had never warmed to, were already there. He was in time to play in the garden with his two grandchildren, a girl of five and a boy of three. He was trying to teach them to catch a tennis ball, and all three of them were delighted with the progress made since their last attempts three months ago.

Presently, they grew too excited under his vigorous encouragement, as their grandmother had known they would. Christine watched with a smile on her face from the kitchen window, as the ball flew in wilder, less predictable arcs and John crawled stiffly between roses and peonies and fiercer things such as pyracantha to retrieve it for the children. He made a good grandad, when he was around. He seemed even to be able to forget his latest murder case, his almost personal desire for justice for this lonely, dead girl, as he gambolled with the children and kept them protectively away from thorns.

The cloud of retirement had lifted from him, for a few hours. They had not mentioned it, since he came home with the news last Wednesday night. But Christine Lambert knew how he was struggling to come to terms with what many men would have welcomed.

The lunch went well. Christine's roast beef was as tender and as tasty as ever, and her Yorkshire pudding brought the usual compliments from her son-in-law, a Yorkshireman by birth, who claimed it was better than anything his own mother had ever produced. They had a bottle of Australian

J. M. Gregson

Shiraz with the meal. Afterwards, the four adults slumped in drowsy contentment in the conservatory with their coffee, whilst the children played on the lawn outside. An idyllic scene of rural contentment, thought Christine. Well, suburban contentment, at any rate.

It was almost three o'clock before she caught John looking at his watch. That must surely be a record.

It was a bleak Sunday for Malcolm Flynn. The tiny square of unchanging blue sky which was all that was visible through the one small, high window of his cell only made the day seem darker for him.

He heard the people he had been supplying taken up for interview, one by one during the morning. They would be charged with possession and dealing, would probably get a year or two inside, depending on their previous criminal records. He was ready for the police to come down for him and take him up to the interview room, but it did not happen. Perhaps even Drugs Squad officers wanted their Sunday afternoons off. But the thought that they might come for him, together with speculation about what the three dealers arrested with him might have said in their interviews, kept him on edge.

Malcolm knew already the tactics he must adopt. He would give away nothing of what he knew about the system, about the hierarchy above him in this well-drilled organization. He didn't know very much anyway, and revelations would bring swift retribution. Inside prison or out, the barons made sure that death came swiftly to those who did not preserve their anonymity.

He wouldn't go for bail. He would be safer in custody than outside, now that he had been caught. There was no sentiment with the men who controlled this lucrative trade: they were likely to eliminate someone who had been caught, sometimes for no better reason than to avoid the

134

unwelcome publicity of a court case. He had the name of the company's brief, who would do his best for him without giving anything away about people higher up the line. This man would tell him just what he could and could not say in court.

By five o'clock, Malcolm Flynn had decided that no one would see him before Monday morning. They had given him a much better lunch than he had expected in a place like this. He tried to look forward to the next meal as the landmark in a day which was stretching interminably. Might as well get used to being bored. He was going to be locked up for years, whatever the mitigating circumstances his brief could dig up. The square of sky above him, remote and unattainable through the high, small window, was still an unbroken blue.

He was trying to doze when he heard the bolts being noisily drawn back on the outside of his cell door. The bored station sergeant took him up to the interview room, refusing to answer any of his queries.

A tall man with grizzled hair, whom he had never seen before, came into the room and studied him for a moment before he sat down, as if the man opposite him was something scraped off his shoe. Par for the course, that, with the fuzz: it didn't unnerve Malcolm. If this pig was Drugs Squad, he must be part of the hierarchy, who stayed safe at his desk rather than going out into the field. Some bigwig sent in to quiz the latest capture. A man of his rank would only come in on a Sunday for quite a big fish. Malcolm felt a small, perverted pride in his criminal status.

The copper set the tape in motion, announced his name as Superintendent Lambert, and added the name of the uniformed constable who sat watchfully behind him. Then he said, 'Well, Mr Flynn, you've landed yourself with a big one, here. Street value of well over a hundred thousand,

I'm told, and caught passing it to three of your dealers. Red-handed, apparently.'

There was something not quite right here, something about that 'I'm told' and that 'apparently' that didn't sound right, as if this man was distancing himself from the charges that had already been laid against Malcolm. He felt that extra tinge of unease which always comes with the unknown. He said, 'I don't say anything about those charges without my brief present.'

'Very wise, if I may say so. But I'm not here about all that. I wanted a more informal chat.' Lambert gave a slight smile to the uncomprehending face and then rapped out, 'About something much more serious!'

Malcolm felt a chill in his veins. But he put on the boldest front he could. 'I'm glad to hear it. Most people seem to think supplying drugs that will be legal in a few years quite serious.'

Lambert smiled at him, until Malcolm felt like a mouse whose every move will be covered by the cat calling the shots. 'Class A drugs will never be legal, and you know it. But drugs aren't my concern, Flynn, I'm glad to say. I'm sure you'll get what's coming to you in due course. This is something much juicier. Murder.' He stared at his man, not disguising his interest in the reaction the word might bring.

He was not disappointed. Malcolm Flynn, who had prepared himself to stonewall on the drugs issue, was visibly shaken. He knew suddenly what was coming. That damned girl! But he wasn't going to give anything away. He had been questioned by pigs before. He knew that you had to keep your wits about you, to give them nothing they didn't have already. He forced a twisted smile, said calmly, 'I don't know what you're talking about. I haven't killed anyone.'

'Kate Wharton, Flynn.'

'Don't even know the girl.'

'Her body was found on the golf course at Ross-on-Wye last Monday, She'd been killed on the previous day.'

'I read about it. But I don't know why you should bother to come in here to talk to me about the girl. I certainly didn't know her.'

Lambert smiled at him: their faces were barely two feet apart, as he leaned forward, with only the small square table between them. 'A lie, that. And we've got it on tape. Won't look too good for you, on top of other things. You could talk yourself into a murder charge, if we go on like this.'

'I didn't kill the girl!' He hadn't meant to shout like that, as if he was panicking. They liked it if you panicked. Malcolm said more quietly, but with the conviction draining from his voice, 'I told you, I didn't even know her.'

'This is disappointing, Flynn. I would have expected more co-operation, from a man in your position. But of course, if you killed the girl, you've nowhere to go, have you? Might as well carry on denying it, I suppose, and hope we can't assemble the evidence to lock you away. But we will, you know, if you did it. Might take us a few days, but you're not going anywhere, are you? With serious drugs charges against you, we can take our time about the murder charge.' Lambert nodded quietly to himself, as though confirming his satisfaction with the situation.

Malcolm felt fear welling behind his eyes, where it must surely show to this unexpected tormentor. The picture of him locked away like a rat in here, whilst the police patiently built a case against him, filled him with horror. He said stubbornly, 'I didn't even know the girl.'

Lambert studied him for a moment, enjoying the trapped look on his face. 'You knew her all right. She was one of your dealers. We can bring witnesses to that, whenever we need them.'

Malcolm thought quickly. Perhaps those three they had

arrested with him last night had talked. Or perhaps the girl herself had been to the police, between the row when she had walked out of the system and her death. Concede it then, but give them as little as possible. 'All right, I did know her,' he admitted. 'She dealt a bit for me. But it's a long time since I saw her.'

Lambert smiled again. 'That's better, Flynn. But not a lot better. You're still being distinctly economical with the truth. It's less than a fortnight since you saw Kate Wharton, isn't it?'

Of course, they must have been on to him long before they arrested him last night: they had known all about last night's drop with his three dealers, had let him walk into a trap. They must have been watching him for weeks. For months, probably. As the knowledge tumbled suddenly in upon him, he said dully, 'I don't remember. I was sure it was longer than that.'

'Let's stop playing games, shall we? You were seen with Kate Wharton in a pub near the Gloucester docks, on the night of Monday, 30th April. You were seen to have a fierce argument with her, in fact. We believe that she was refusing to deal, refusing to have anything further to do with your operation.'

Malcolm wondered how much more they knew, how much more this man was going to release to him in dribs and drabs. 'She did refuse to deal,' he concurred. 'That was the last time I saw her.'

'Except for when you killed her, of course.'

'I didn't!' His shout was so loud that the constable started forward automatically, as if to defend his superintendent. Lambert held up a hand without taking his eyes from his opponent's face as Flynn continued urgently, 'I've never killed anyone in my life. Never even been involved in violence.'

Lambert studied the flat-featured, terrified face for a

moment before he said, 'Not personally, perhaps. But we know the way your organization operates as well as you do. Perhaps better. You pass the information up the hierarchy. People who want to leave don't have that option: they are simply eliminated. Usually by a contract killer – nothing so crude as you having to do the job yourself. It's kept impersonal and efficient. But when you passed the information upstairs, you knew you were killing Kate Wharton, as certainly as if you had tightened that cord around her neck yourself.'

'I didn't kill the girl! All right, I passed on the information that she wanted out, but that was as far as it went. I didn't know what would happen to her. And I'd no choice in the matter – I had to report that she was trying to opt out!'

Lambert watched the frightened man with distaste. He had no pity for him; Flynn was intelligent enough to know the effects of the evil goods he purveyed. But what he said was true enough. The drugs system operated rather like Stalin's secret police: if you withheld any information, if you did not pass it upwards immediately, you were likely to be liquidated yourself, as unreliable. 'When did you tell your immediate superior about Kate Wharton?' he asked.

'Wednesday night. It was the first opportunity I had.'

Lambert didn't press him for names. Possibly Flynn himself didn't know even the name of the man above him, in the massive secrecy which cloaked the higher echelons of the organization. That was Drugs Squad business, for tomorrow. 'What happened then?'

'I've no idea. The next thing I heard about Kate Wharton was when I read in the papers that she was dead.'

'I advise you to tell the truth for once, as you've conspicuously avoided doing whenever you could. You don't wish to change your story about Wednesday night? You're certain that's when you passed on the information?'

139

'Yes. And the last time I saw the girl was two nights before that.' He was desperately anxious now to be believed, desperate to convince them.

Lambert thought for a moment, without taking his eyes off his quarry's face. It made sense. If Flynn had passed the information upwards on Wednesday night, the timing was about right. The organization would have brought in a contract killer, who would have sized up his designated victim and the right opportunity to dispatch her. Four days was about right for this, enabling the anonymous killer to isolate his victim and dump her body on the Sunday night.

He stood up. 'If you come up with anything else, pass it on immediately. There's a murder rap waiting here, for someone. Try to make sure it's not you, if you really didn't do it.'

Malcolm Flynn was not bored that evening. He was too troubled for that. His unexpected visitor left him tossing miserably from side to side throughout the night on the unyielding bunk in the cell.

Fourteen

Richard Ellacott enjoyed Monday mornings. He thought it was the best time of the week for the Captain of Oldford Golf Club.

He played with the seniors on Mondays, all men over sixty, most of them over seventy, and with a good sprinkling of sprightly octogenarians. At sixty-two, he was a youngster, and he enjoyed that. He had his own tee-off time at nine o'clock, and the tradition was that members fell back and allowed the Captain precedence, on the course and off it. If his match caught up with another one, he must never be kept waiting, but waved through, while the players in the match in front of him stood back and smiled. It was a harmless piece of deference, to emphasize that the Captain of the club was in charge of all golfing matters, that he was king for a year before he retreated back to the ranks, like other men before him.

Richard shrugged away this half-serious veneration of his office, pretended to be a little embarrassed by it. But you couldn't help liking it, really, he told his mirror, as he brushed his grey but still plentiful hair and combed his moustache. Many of these seniors had fought in the 1939–45 War, whereas Richard was just young enough to have missed even National Service. And here were these heroes deferring to him on the golf course!

He was playing a challenge match with the pro today

141

against two members, one of a series the Captain tradition-
ally undertook throughout his year. The match would be
keenly contested, but the result did not really matter that
much. There would be much cheerful banter in the bar
afterwards, when the losers would be ribbed by the rest
of the seniors. Monday morning at Oldford was largely
an all-male preserve, with hearty men's laughter, broad
humour, little malice, and an indulgence of the schoolboy
that is still close to the surface in most healthy men.

Richard had already showered, dressed and breakfasted.
He glanced at the alarm clock by his bed before he went
to clean his teeth. It was quarter past eight. He was only
ten minutes' drive from the club. He had plenty of time.
He would get there by twenty to nine, change his shoes in
the locker room, enjoy the greetings of 'Good morning, Mr
Captain!' and the bluff male badinage of the locker room
before he strolled out to the busy Monday morning tee and
watched the ranks of senior golfers fall back obediently
with their trolleys to allow his passage.

He took the tray with the pot of tea and the toast into the
room of his invalid wife. 'Might be a bit late back again,
dear,' he said, as she struggled to a sitting position and
he plumped the pillows behind her. 'You know what it's
like, being Captain. You can't just get away when you
like. You're the servant of the members, for your year
of office.'

It was a formula he had been repeating since he became
Captain at the beginning of the year, but she didn't mind.
She knew he was enjoying it, and it was important for a
man who didn't get all the comforts at home – which he
had once enjoyed – to relish his life outside. 'I'll be all
right,' she said. 'I'll get up in a little while, get myself
a little lunch in due course. I might be able to sit in the
garden later, if the sun stays out.'

She accepted his peck on the cheek, gave him an

encouraging smile as he left, then sank back exhausted into the pillows. She would tackle the toast in a minute, when she'd got her strength back. The MS had got much worse, during these last twelve months: even the drugs didn't seem to hold it at bay as effectively now as they had done in previous years.

But Richard was very kind, very patient, most of the time. Now that he was semi-retired from his accountancy business, it was good that he had the diversions of the golf club. She was sorry she didn't feel up to attending the social occasions herself any more. But Richard seemed to be enjoying them, especially in this year of the captaincy: he was at the club on quite a lot of nights, as well as playing during the days. Perhaps he would find a new partner for himself at the golf club, when she was gone.

No use being morbid. She sat up, turned on the bedside radio, and poured herself a cup of tea.

Richard had put his bag with his change of clothes for after the game into the car and was ready to go out when the phone rang. He went quickly into his study and picked it up. 'Richard Ellacott here. I'm afraid I haven't much time, because I'm about to—'

'You've time for this. It won't take long.'

A neutral voice, female, he was sure, but muffled. It sent a chill racing up his spine. 'Who is this? I told you, I—'

'I know about Kate Wharton.'

His head reeled. He said desperately, 'Kate who? I think you must have the wrong number, and I really haven't—'

'The girl you paid to sleep with you, Richard Ellacott. Many times. Too many, as it turns out. The girl who was murdered, a week ago.'

He tried desperately to think who this might be, but he had no idea. The voice was deliberately even, deliberately deadened. He wanted to slam the receiver down, to stalk out of his house with his head held high. Instead, he found himself saying, 'What is it you want with me?'

The voice did not immediately reply, and he wondered if the silence was itself a tactic. Then it said, 'The police know about you and Kate, Richard. Your name was in the back of her diary.'

He felt the blood pounding in his temples. 'I've no reason to fear the police. I didn't kill Kate Wharton.'

Another pause, even more agonizing, as he waited for a reaction. He was almost certain he caught a vestige of a chuckle before the voice resumed its flatness: 'That's as may be. But I don't think your wife would be happy to hear you'd been making regular visits to a prostitute. Or the people who work for you. Or your chums at the golf club, for that matter.'

He wanted to tell the voice to go to hell. Publish and be damned, the Duke of Wellington had said. But Richard wasn't the Iron Duke, and he knew it. He could not force the outrage he intended into his voice as he demanded, 'Who the hell are you? And what are you proposing to do?'

Another of those excruciating pauses. Then the voice said, 'You had an – an arrangement with Kate, didn't you, Richard?'

'She was blackmailing me, you mean, don't you? If you think I'm going to—'

'A thousand pounds, last time, I think. I don't see why that shouldn't be continued. With a different receiver, of course.'

'But look, I can't afford—'

'Oh, I think you can, Richard. With as much at stake as you have. But there's good news for you, as well as bad. Just a one-off payment, it will be, and then you'll be rid of this for ever.'

He licked dry lips. 'How much?'

'Two thousand. Very reasonable, really, for a final, one-off payment.'

But it never was, was it? Blackmailers always came back for more, people said. And there were no photographic negatives he could exchange for his payment, no evidence which would not be there just as clearly as a weapon against him after this two thousand pounds had gone. He had thought the nightmare had been concluded with the death of Kate Wharton. Now he heard himself saying, 'You promise that? One payment, and then it's finished?'

'Finished for ever, Richard.' The flat voice was suddenly persuasive.

He felt utterly defeated, as though his replies were now dictated for him by this voice he could not identify on the other end of the line. 'It will take me a couple of days to get the money.'

'Let's say Thursday night, then. I don't want to be unreasonable.'

'Where?'

'The old patch. Where you used to pick up Kate. Ten o'clock. Stop your car. I'll be waiting.'

'All right. This will finish it once and for all, though.'

'Of course it will, Richard Ellacott.' The voice had dropped its impersonal tone, now, but he still could not recognize it. It rolled his full name off its tongue, seeming to savour each syllable.

He looked at the dashboard clock as he slid into the driving seat of his car. He didn't have plenty of time any more. But that no longer mattered. He knew as he drove to the club that he would lose this morning's match, that the lunch-time banter would clog his distracted ears, that his joking replies would sit like ashes in his mouth.

In the phone booth in Gloucester, Tracey Boyd unwound her old tights from the mouthpiece and relaxed. She'd been right about where Kate had got that extra thousand from.

And blackmail had been easier than she had expected, in the end.

Roy Cook's house was in one of the small villages on the edge of the Forest of Dean. It was the end of what had once been a terrace of council houses. Two thirds of them were now privately owned, including this one, crouched beneath the shoulder of the hill as if it were seeking shelter from the winter winds.

It was half-past nine when they got there, and this on the morning of the fourteenth of May, but the sun was only just beginning to touch the roof of the house, so abruptly did the hill rise to the north-east behind it. Oak and beech had been in leaf as they drove into the forest, but this was a high valley and the buds on the trees beside the house were only just breaking.

Cook stood in the doorway of the house before Lambert and Hook were properly out of the car, his powerful figure seeming even larger against the shadows behind him. He nodded to them without a smile as they walked up the path which bisected the long, narrow front garden. He motioned them into the house, then looked out upon the quiet scene before him and glanced along the frontage of the terrace to his left, as if he wished to convince himself that no one was taking an interest in these visitors of his.

'Peaceful spot you've found for yourself here,' Lambert remarked, as they looked out over a rear garden dominated by neat rows of potatoes, onions and newly planted brassicas.

'I like it.'

He was tense, waiting for them to start on the business of this visit, and Lambert, noticing this, perversely decided to prolong his tension. 'I'm sorry if you've had to take a morning off work. We'd have come to see you in the woods again, you know, if that had been easier for you.'

'They owe me. I don't take my full holiday allowance, anyway.' He hadn't wanted CID coming to see him at his place of work again, not with Julie telling him what they knew about him now. There had been enough gossip about the last visit by his fellow-workers, whose featureless lives made a CID visit a matter of major interest. When you had a background like Roy Cook's, you learned to keep such things as quiet as possible. Anyway, if he claimed a doctor's appointment and went in as soon as these two had finished with him, he probably wouldn't be docked for the morning. No need to tell them that.

Lambert said, 'I expect Mrs Wharton told you about our visit to her house on Saturday.'

'She mentioned it, yes.' She'd been through it with him in detail, twice, and insisted on discussing what his tactics should be when they made their inevitable contact with him. He hadn't wanted to talk about it with her. He didn't see any point in reviving the scene which had made him leave her house, which had stopped them sleeping with each other for three months, until their lust had brought them back together again, so that their first frenzied couplings had made the separation seem almost worthwhile.

Roy felt he wasn't a good liar, not to an intelligent woman like Julie, and he had deliberately avoided any discussion of what had happened to Kate in the years after she had left. But Julie hadn't seemed to notice, so anxious had she been to work out with him what he should say now. She'd been disappointed when he'd refused to stay the night with her, but he had insisted on coming back to what she had taken to calling his bolt-hole, where no one was interested in the loner who made only occasional visits to the village pub.

Lambert continued: 'We were interested in your assault upon Kate Wharton. We have to be interested in anything which concerns a relationship with a dead girl.'

147

'It was four years ago. It had nothing to do with Kate's death.'

'Perhaps. But you chose to conceal it from us, when we spoke on Friday in the forest.' He hadn't disputed the word assault, Lambert noticed.

Cook shrugged his massive shoulders, dropped his dark eyes to the faded carpet between him and the two men for whom his small sofa seemed scarcely adequate. 'It's not something to be proud of, is it? It almost finished Julie and me, that did.'

'Mrs Wharton said she blames herself, to some extent. Kate was an attractive girl of eighteen, in short skirts, and she should have foreseen trouble, she said.'

Rather to their surprise, he did not seize on the easy excuse, as most men would have done. 'I should have had more sense, shouldn't I? I should have listened when the girl said no. But like the bloody fool I am, I thought she could be persuaded. She was a prick-teaser was Kate, whether she meant to be or not. She went on the game after she'd left home, you know.'

'We do know that, yes. But at the moment I'm more interested in the reasons she left home than what she did afterwards.'

Roy thought that was hopeful. He tried not to show it in his face. He tried to think exactly what Julie and he had agreed he should say. It wasn't as easy as he had expected to deliver words they had carefully worked out together. Acting came into it, and he had never tried to act. 'I'm sure there were other reasons, besides me,' he suggested.

That was too weak, not the line they had agreed at all. He had lost his way already.

As if he divined that, Lambert said, 'But your assault was the main reason, it seems.'

'I suppose so.' It was all going wrong. The truth seemed

to be coming out, because he found he couldn't just parrot out the phrases Julie had prepared for him.

'It was more than just a pass at a pretty girl, wasn't it, Mr Cook?'

It was the very phrase Julie had told him to use, to make light of the incident. Yet he found he couldn't bring himself to insist upon it, now. It was a phrase he had never used in his life, and he was sure that these watchful, experienced men would know that, would be amused by his clumsy attempts at deceit, if he came out with it here. He said lamely, 'No. It was nothing much, really.'

'It was more than nothing much, wasn't it? A lot more, in fact.'

'All right!' The big fists clenched and unclenched in his anger, and this time he did make himself use one of the phrases they had agreed upon. 'I misread the signals, that was all. Went a bit further than I should have done.'

'Just the same as you did with Janice Brown in South London?'

He started forward on his upright chair as though he would hit his questioner, but Lambert did not move. Cook sank back again, looked at the carpet and muttered, 'Trust the bloody pigs to bring that up. I was never bloody charged with that, you know.'

'We do know, yes. We also know why. It was because the woman you raped lost her nerve and wouldn't go into court to testify. Was that what happened with Kate Wharton, Mr Cook? Did she lose her nerve and—'

'I didn't rape Kate!' He shouted the denial, his careful phrases flying out of his brain, his only aim to stop this man spewing his accusations. 'I was nowhere near raping Kate!'

'Interrupted, were you, Mr Cook? The girl's mother came in before it could get any worse, did she?'

It was pure conjecture, but it struck home. It seemed

to Roy Cook that Julie must have revealed more than she said she had, perhaps more than she believed she had, to these persistent, watchful men who were so much better with words than he was. He said, 'It was a bit like that, I suppose. Julie came in when I – when we – were just—'

'Kate's mother came in just in time to stop you, didn't she? When the girl was resisting, screaming probably, and you weren't prepared to take no for an answer.'

'Something like that.' He felt relief rather than dismay that it was out at last, that he no longer had to play these word games he could not manage. He wondered if they would demand every sordid detail of a scene still vivid in his mind after this forced recollection.

But Lambert was satisfied with the admission. What Cook did not know was that this was primarily a softening-up process for what was to follow. 'With your record, with time inside for assault upon a woman, I think you were very lucky to be interrupted when you were. You were also extraordinarily fortunate that Kate Wharton decided not to press charges of indecent assault at least.'

'All right, all right! You've had what you want. There's no need to rub my nose in it! It cost me enough at the time.' Roy Cook was suddenly aware of what he had given away, of how far he had strayed from Julie's careful briefing.

It was Bert Hook, looking up from his notebook, who said, as if merely seeking confirmation for the record, 'So Kate Wharton left home as a result of this incident. And Julie Wharton threw you out of her house.'

It was so far from what he and Julie had agreed that he was reluctant to confirm it. But that secret had disappeared with the rest when he was unable to mouth the phrases they had agreed. He muttered, 'Something like that, yes.'

'I see.' Hook made a careful note in his round hand, whilst the silence built in the small, sparsely furnished room. 'And when did you next see Kate Wharton, Mr Cook?'

The bombshell was dropped so quietly that Roy Cook did not hear it for what it was at first. Before he realized that he was committing himself, he said gruffly, 'That wasn't for some time. Not until I'd got back with Julie. Not until I'd been back with Julie for over a year.'

His last statements were a desperate attempt to direct the exchanges back to safe ground, back to his relationship with Julie Wharton and away from her dead daughter.

But it was too late. Lambert came back in, taking up the thread of the dialogue from the sergeant, who looked so harmless, who had just trapped Roy Cook into the most damaging admission he could have made. 'So how long after your assault upon Kate Wharton did you renew acquaintance with her?'

Roy hated that last phrase, hated being patronized by these men. But he was not stupid, despite his performance today. He realized now that if he tried to bandy words with this man he would come off worse, that his best policy was to say as little as possible. Whether they had known about his dealings with Kate Wharton before they came here was beside the point – they knew now, because of his own crassness. Therefore limit the damage: pretend to be honest, but give them as little as you can.

'Probably eighteen months after she'd left home. Maybe as long as two years. I can't be sure. I'd been back with Julie for well over a year, but I kept this place on. I stay the night often enough there, but—'

'And why did you visit Kate?'

He was back on dangerous ground. But at least he wasn't inhibited by those prearranged phrases, those notions framed in words he would never have used himself. He said cautiously, 'She was on the game by then. I'd heard about it. Seen her myself, one night. We had unfinished business.' That was the phrase Kate had used herself, the first time he had picked her up. He didn't realize how chilling it seemed now, coming from his uncertain lips in this quiet room.

'You visited Kate and paid her for sex?'

'Yes.' He'd assumed they'd known that. Now he wasn't sure that he needed to have given the information away so easily.

'And Kate Wharton didn't object to that?'

From a man who's almost raped her, they meant. And there had been a bit of difficulty, the first time, until he'd convinced her a tart had to take everyone's money, without picking and choosing. 'No. She was a tart, wasn't she?'

'Apparently she was, yes. So she took your money like everyone else's. How often?'

'Not that often. Half a dozen times, perhaps, over the last couple of years.'

'And what does her mother think about these visits?'

Lambert had thrown in the unexpected question again, and caught him unprepared for it. Roy had assumed this was like other conversations between men, where the assumption was that the wife or partner didn't know, and would never be told. 'Julie doesn't know,' he stressed. 'And you mustn't bloody tell her!'

'You're hardly in a position to lay down the rules, are you, Mr Cook? If it affects a murder investigation, if we have any reason to suppose you're holding things back, of course we shall need to question Mrs Wharton about this. If it doesn't affect the outcome of the case, we don't reveal confidential information, but there can be no guarantees.'

Roy saw how bad things must look, how appalled Julie would be if she knew. He couldn't start to explain his sexual curiosity to these impassive men, couldn't explain how he had gloried in the mother's sexual voracity and wondered how the daughter might compare. He couldn't even enlarge on the delights of young flesh to a man of his age: he hadn't the words, and these men wouldn't want to understand, if he had. He produced a word he never used in public. 'I love Julie. I don't want to lose her.'

He wanted to say that monogamy was an unnatural state for a highly sexed man like him, but he didn't even know the word, wouldn't have known how to frame the argument to these grave faces, if he had. He could have put the idea to sympathetic listeners in the pub, after a few pints, but not to these two.

Lambert said dryly, 'Mrs Wharton seems very anxious to protect you. Even at the expense of her dead daughter. You might do well to bear that in mind, if you wish your relationship to continue. But that's not our concern.'

'No, it's mine. I'm keeping out of trouble at work. I'm going to keep out of other women's beds, from now on.'

There was no doubting his earnestness, at that moment. Lambert doubted if it would last for the rest of his life. 'You put yourself in Kate's power, didn't you, visiting her like that?' he questioned.

'She could have told Julie, you mean? But tarts don't, do they? Not when they're on the game. They'd soon get cut up, if they started telling wives.'

'Or brutally strangled with a cord, as in Kate Wharton's case.'

Roy was aware that he had led himself into this, had set up Lambert's comment, but he wasn't quite sure how. He put it down to the fact that they were cleverer and more experienced in these word games than he was. He said dully, 'I didn't kill Kate. I don't know who did.'

'Really. But you agree that you had put yourself in a vulnerable position by visiting Kate and paying her for sex, without the knowledge of her mother. Did she ask you for money to keep her mouth shut?'

'No. Blackmail, you mean? She wouldn't do that, not Kate.'

Lambert wondered whether to tell him that she almost certainly had, and that he had just told them that he was a leading candidate to be her blackmail victim. Instead, he said, 'Kate Wharton never demanded money from you for her silence? Never asked for more than the normal amount for her sexual favours?'

'No. I said Julie mustn't ever know, the very first time we did it.'

For a man who'd done time and wronged women in various ways, he still showed a touching trust in prostitutes. Lambert studied him for a moment, then asked, 'Who do you think killed Kate, Mr Cook?'

'I don't know. Drugs people, I expect. She was a dealer, you know.'

'Not at the time of her death, she wasn't. Did she ever say anything about her dealing, to you?'

'No. She offered me coke once, about a year ago, and I told her to get out while she still could.'

Lambert stood up, watched his man relax a little, then said, 'Those woods where we came to see you on Friday. Dymock Forest, I believe they call that stretch. Work there regularly, do you?'

'We move around, go where we're sent. But I've been working in those woods for the last three months or so. Why?'

'No real reason. Just that there's a car park for people who walk in the forest, not more than a mile from where we saw you.'

He nodded. 'On the lane to Kempley, that's right. What of it?'

'That car park is on the other side of the road from Ross golf course. Within fifty yards of the place where Kate's body was found. It would be a very quiet and convenient place to take a vehicle, late at night. For someone who had to dispose of a body.'

They left him standing in the doorway, pondering on that thought.

Fifteen

R ichard Ellacott was very different from Roy Cook in his attitude to the police. He had been used to meeting quite senior officers on equal terms, was a member of Rotary, a man used to dealing with words and with people.

The call he had expected came at two o'clock, whilst he was still at Oldford Golf Club. Detective Sergeant Hook from the CID was courteous and unexcited. He understood that Mr Ellacott had already spoken to uniformed men during their routine enquiries that were being made at all golf clubs in the area. This was another matter, still routine, but relating to him alone. It was, however, fairly urgent. Superintendent Lambert would come with DS Hook to see him at home, if he preferred it.

Richard said hastily that they could come to the golf club, as soon as they liked. He was only too anxious to help them. They could go into the Committee Room there and be undisturbed. He didn't expect it would take very long. DS Hook didn't respond to that.

Richard explained to the men he was drinking with at the club that the cares of office had struck again. The Captain was required to speak to the police about this murder they'd had up at the Ross-on-Wye club. Boring routine, no doubt, but at least the Captain could shelter his members against it. He would see the fuzz in the Committee Room and

156

rejoin them later. Unless he was led away in handcuffs, of course, ha ha.

His companions had drunk more than he had. Their normally indulgent Captain had been careful this lunchtime, in anticipation of this. He had been drinking merely tonics for the last three rounds. When he brought them the news that he was about to see the CID, there was much noisy hilarity at Ellacott's expense, many offers of prison visiting, of files smuggled in inside cakes. Golf club humour is nothing if not predictable.

Richard was waiting for them in the car park when they arrived in the police Mondeo. He took them into the deserted Committee Room and set them at one side of the big oval table, which could accommodate up to fifteen people when the full committee of the club met. He sat in the chair at the other side where he always sat as Captain, hoping that would increase his confidence.

'We have to ask you some questions about Kate Wharton, Mr Ellacott,' Lambert began.

Richard nodded. 'The girl who was killed last week at Ross golf course.'

'Yes. You know the Ross course, I expect.'

'I do indeed. Not as well as I know this one, of course. I've played there, but not recently. Excellent course!'

'Yes. It seems that whoever dumped the body had chosen his spot quite carefully.'

'I spoke to your officers about that on Friday. They wanted to know if we had anyone in the club who might be a suspect. I've thought about it, and discussed it with some of our most experienced members over the weekend, as I promised them I would. But I haven't come up with any likely names, I'm afraid.'

'I see. Well, thank you for your efforts. We're here today to talk to you about something more specific.'

'Well, fire away! Always glad to be of whatever assistance I can to the arm of the law!' Richard wondered if he
was overdoing the bonhomie, if it was coming through as
false. He found the way this tall man with the unblinking
grey eyes stared at him quite unnerving. He realized now
that he had only met senior policemen in social situations
before, and this was very different.

'Our Scenes of Crime team found a diary amongst the
dead girl's effects at her flat.' Lambert paused for a moment
to see what reaction that information might bring, and
detected surprisingly little reaction in Ellacott, who was
nodding slowly. 'Unfortunately, Kate Wharton hadn't kept
a daily diary. Not many people do, in our experience. But
she had recorded three names on a sheet at the back of this
little book. One of them was Richard Ellacott.'

Richard found his heart pounding, even as he raised his
eyebrows in mock surprise. 'There are other Ellacotts,
Superintendent.'

'But only one other one in the Gloucester and District
telephone directory. And he has no R in his initials.'

Richard glanced automatically at the door to make sure
it was closed, then was furious with himself for the
movement. He had already decided that there was only
one way to play this, and nervousness wouldn't improve
his performance. He gave them what he thought of as his
frankest smile, then said, 'Look here, can I rely on your
discretion?'

Lambert allowed himself the ghost of a smile at this
question, which invariably prefaced a disclosure of some
kind. 'I think you know the answer to that, Mr Ellacott.
We're always as discreet as we can be about what we learn,
but if it has a bearing on a serious crime, there can be no
guarantees.'

'Yes, I see that, of course. Well, I've more to lose than
most, I suppose. I have an invalid wife at home, five people

158

who work for me in my firm, and I'm the Captain of this golf club.'

They didn't have any doubt that the last of these milieus was the one where he most feared exposure. He waited for some comforting reply, then realized that Lambert had said all he was going to offer in the way of reassurance.

Richard nodded two or three times to himself, then said, 'I'll rely on your discretion, then. I'm sure you won't reveal anything you don't have to, and hopefully when you arrest this girl's killer all this will be decently buried.' He licked his lips, waited again for a comment from either of the men, who listened to him so carefully, and found once more that none was forthcoming. 'I expect you will know by now that Kate was a prostitute.'

'Yes. We are following up as many of her clients as we can discover. Statistically, there's a better than fifty per cent chance that one of them killed her.' Lambert turned the screw a little further, his face inscrutable.

'Really? Well, I suppose that would be so, up and down the country, when you think about it. Look, I'm not proud of this, but I have to tell you that I was one of Kate Wharton's clients! Which is not to say that I killed her, of course!' His laugh rang unnaturally loud around the big room, with its panels on the walls listing the names of the club's trophy winners over the years.

'I'm glad to hear it. Regular visitor to Miss Wharton, were you, Mr Ellacott?'

Richard wondered whether the frequency of his visits made him more or less likely to have killed her. They would probably give him the statistics of that, in a minute. 'I suppose I was, yes, eventually.'

'How often did you see her?'

'Look, Superintendent, I said I wasn't proud of this. You should know something about the circumstances. My wife has multiple sclerosis, which has been developing over the years. It's reached the point where—'

Lambert held up his hand. 'I'm sorry about that, but we really don't need any details. We're not here to arbitrate on morals, but to investigate a murder. People's private lives are no business of ours, except where they have a bearing on that murder investigation.'

'Yes. Yes, of course. It's just that I've never had to admit to anything like this before, and it doesn't come easy. Well, let me be completely frank. I picked Kate Wharton up on the street, the first two times. She was a very pretty girl, as you will know. A cut above most of the others who practise her trade. She made it clear she'd only do straight sex, but that was all right with me, that was all I wanted. Getting a bit long in the tooth to be swinging from the chandeliers!' Richard realized as soon as the words were out that his attempt at humour had been ill-judged. But his laugh came again, automatic and brief, sounding in his ears as though it came from someone else, some buffoon outside the window.

'How often were you seeing her, Mr Ellacott?'

'I was coming to that. After the first two occasions, when I picked her up on the street and she took me back to her flat, I suggested that I would go straight to the flat, at a time convenient to both of us. That is what I did after that. She was a pleasant as well as a pretty girl, and not unintelligent. I like to think we became quite good friends, eventually.'

The familiar, pathetic claim of the ageing Lothario who paid for sex: it wasn't just a commercial transaction, she had feelings for me. Lambert controlled a sigh and said impatiently, 'How often, Mr Ellacott?'

'Once a week, these last months. I told you, we became quite good friends.' It was important for him to emphasize that, if they were going to raise what he thought they were.

'I see. When did you last see her?'

'On the Tuesday evening before she died.'

'The first of May.'

'Yes, that would be the date.'

'Did you usually see her on Tuesdays?'

'More often than not, yes. Sometimes it was in the afternoons, if I could make it then.'

Which would leave Kate Wharton free to ply her dubious trade in the evenings, if she chose. This man must have been one of her better customers, being both regular in his visits and accommodating about the times. Perhaps they had become friends of a sort, exchanged the odd confidence. Some prostitutes did well by being good listeners, though they rarely volunteered much about themselves. 'I want you to consider that last meeting carefully. Did Miss Wharton seem to be upset or frightened about anything?' Lambert asked.

Richard took his time, as he had been bidden. He could divert suspicion away from himself here, if he was careful. 'Kate did seem a bit preoccupied, on that last Tuesday. I think I know why, too.'

'Then you'd better give us all the information you can.'

'She'd been a pusher for drugs. Do you know that?'

'Yes. She'd been both a user – though never an addict – and a dealer.'

'Well, you may know more than I do. But she was worried, the last time I saw her, and when I pressed her a little about it, she told me why. She'd told the man who supplied her that she wasn't going to be a pusher any more, that she was getting out of the trade altogether.' Richard tried unsuccessfully to look modest. 'I'd been encouraging her to do that, when we had our little talks.'

And when she took your advice, she might have signed her death warrant, thought Lambert. But you couldn't blame this well-meaning, slightly pathetic man for that. Cutting herself off from all contact with hard drugs had been the right thing for Kate Wharton to do. She had needed support and protection, that was all; this man could never have offered her either of those, and perhaps no one could have saved her, if her death was a result of her refusing to trade. 'But you say that she seemed worried on that last Tuesday?'

'Worried and apprehensive. She'd told her supplier that she was giving up dealing drugs on the previous evening, apparently, and she was frightened of what the consequences would be.' This big, experienced man seemed suddenly on the verge of tears. 'She was right about that, wasn't she?'

'Perhaps she was. We aren't certain of that yet.' But Ellacott was almost certainly telling the truth here. They knew that she had told Malcolm Flynn on the previous evening that she wasn't accepting supplies from him any more, that that was the time when she had announced that she was severing her ties with the trade. 'Did she give you any names, mention whom she was scared of?'

'No. She said it wasn't my problem and she would deal with it herself.'

'I see. Why do you think your name was recorded in her diary, Mr Ellacott?'

It was a sudden switch to the key area, and it almost caught Richard off guard. He tried not to show anything more than puzzlement in his face as he said, 'I've no idea. Perhaps – well, perhaps she was just listing her best clients. Her most regular people, I mean.' He had almost said 'favourite' then. But he mustn't appear too sentimental, or they wouldn't think he was objective.

'We've already contacted the other two names. They didn't visit her anything like as frequently as you did.'

Richard wondered whether the other two were in the

same position as him, wondered for the first time whether he had not been the only one to be exploited. 'In that case, I have no suggestions. I can't think why my name should have been there, let alone theirs.'

'There is a possible reason we have to explore. When we are investigating a murder, we have access to all kinds of information which would normally be private, as you probably know. So we have been studying Kate Wharton's bank and building society accounts. A fortnight before she died, she made a deposit of one thousand pounds, which was additional to her normal deposits. Have you any idea how she might have come by a sum like that?'

Richard found he was surprisingly calm, now that the moment had come at last. 'No. She didn't mention anything of that sort to me.'

'Mr Ellacott, all of the three names in the back of that diary are affluent men: certainly they must have seemed so to a girl like Kate Wharton. She might have thought that one or more of them were capable of paying her a little more than the standard rate she charged for her sexual services. In return, perhaps, for the sort of discretion we were talking about earlier.'

He looked suitably shocked. 'Blackmail, you mean? A thousand pounds to keep her mouth shut about visits to a prostitute? No. I wouldn't think Kate would ever be a blackmailer. And she certainly never asked me for money like that. I told you, we had become quite good friends.' He was glad he had played that up now.

Lambert looked at him, assessing his reliability, making no attempt to disguise the fact. 'That thousand pounds came from somewhere, Mr Ellacott.'

'Well, it wasn't from me, I'm glad to say.'

Lambert and Hook stood up, as if operated by the same mechanism. 'That seems to be it, then. Have you any idea how Kate Wharton might have died, Mr Ellacott?'

'None at all, I'm afraid. I've been cudgelling my brains about it ever since I heard the news, of course, but I haven't come up with anything. I should have thought it was the drugs people, myself, but you obviously haven't been able to pin it on anyone from that dubious industry, or you wouldn't be here now.'

Richard thought he had acted it out quite well, really. He went outside and saw them off, stood watching the Mondeo wind its way out of the car park, nodding to a couple of members by the first tee as he felt his world returning to normal. He felt the presence of the Secretary at his side.

'Routine stuff,' he said, in response to the unspoken question. 'Quite boring, really, but at least I was able to take it off your shoulders. I think I convinced them it couldn't have been one of our members who killed that girl. They seem pretty baffled, I'm afraid.'

Roy Cook was shaken by his own weakness. He should have been able to deal with those CID men better. He had been interrogated by police in the past, had always succeeded in giving little away. The situation had been more straightforward then, and he had done little more than maintain a sullen silence, but the fuzz had always had to work hard for anything they got from Roy Cook.

This time it had been different. These men had come to him in his own house, had somehow succeeded in persuading him that they knew more than they did. They had made no bones about the fact that he had become a suspect in a murder case, and he had never had to contend with that before. It had all seemed rather odd to him: not like the police grillings he had endured in London, where nothing he said had been accepted, but more like a normal conversation. Perhaps he was just out of touch: it was a long time since he had had any trouble with the police. He had a regular job and a good woman, and he didn't want to lose either of those.

When he got home from his work in the forest that night, he decided he wouldn't go over to Julie's place. He really couldn't face her today, after what he'd told the police about Kate. He would ring her and tell her he was too tired, in a little while, when he had composed himself and got the words ready.

But his phone was ringing as he opened the front door of the small house, and he went and answered it without thinking of the consequences. It was Julie, as a moment's thought might have told him it would be, anxious to know how his meeting with the CID had gone.

'All right, I think,' he said. It had been anything but all right, but the last thing he wanted to tell her was that they had wormed out of him the fact that he had been visiting her daughter. 'They still don't seem to have any idea who killed Kate,' he told her, with some satisfaction. Then he realized that he was speaking to the mother of a murdered girl, and added lamely, 'I expect they'll get the man who did it in the end, won't they?'

There was a silence at the other end of the line. Then Julie said, 'Did they accept what we'd agreed about Kate? That it wasn't anything much, the incident in this house? Did they accept the idea that it was something very minor, that she'd left home for a whole variety of reasons?'

He stared at the phone for a moment, appalled by how much further he had gone than that with the quiet, persuasive Lambert. He wondered how much he could get away with concealing from Julie. 'No, m'dear. They didn't buy that, I don't think. They didn't seem to accept that I'd just made a bit of a pass at her.' He had managed to produce the phrase at last, when it was no good, when all he was doing was relaying it back to the woman who had devised it for him in the first place.

'So you told them you'd made a full-scale rape attempt on Kate.'

He could hear the anger in her voice. 'I didn't tell them that, no, love. Not in so many words. It was just that they seemed to know all about it already, before they spoke to me. Perhaps you gave away a bit more than you thought to them.'

'I didn't. You should have just stonewalled, as we agreed.' She could see him, the great, stupid, loveable bear of a man, stumbling over the replies they had agreed, becoming ever more confused with those clever pigs. 'Anyway, they can't make anything of it, if you don't let them. You haven't seen her for four years, and that's too long a time for a straightforward man like you to be plotting revenge.'

'Yes. They seem to have me in the frame for it, though.' He wondered how he was ever going to conceal from her the fact that he had seen Kate in those last four years. Seen her the week before last, in fact, just before she died. 'They threw my previous record at me,' he explained.

'Of course they did. We knew that was coming. It's the only reason why they'd be interested in you, isn't it?'

'Yes.' But he knew it wasn't. And the police knew, now.

'Anyway, you can tell me the full story, when you get here. What time do you expect to be over?'

'I was going to tell you. I'm knackered, so I thought I wouldn't come over tonight. I'll come straight there from work tomorrow, instead. I wouldn't be much use in the sack to a demanding woman like you tonight!'

It was a heavy-handed attempt at humour, and it didn't bring the chuckle he had hoped for from the anxious woman at the other end of the line. 'It's not just about sex, is it, Roy?' she said quietly. 'We're more to each other than that. We should be together, at a time like this.'

166

It was true, and for a moment he was tempted. Then the thought of having to conceal his visits to Kate came back, and he replied heavily, 'Not tonight, m'dear. I told you, I'm knackered. Must have taken more out of me than I thought, seeing those CID men. And I been on heavy work all afternoon, handling the chain saw. I just don't fancy the drive, tonight. And I got things to do here.'

Julie Wharton put the phone down thoughtfully after their final endearments. What things? she wondered. And Roy had never made the drive an excuse for not coming over before.

Sixteen

Joe Ashton had got his job back at Sainsbury's. He had got a fierce bollocking from Mr Harding, the store manager, about disappearing for a week without letting anyone know why. Joe stood like a schoolboy with his thin arms at his sides and his head cast down, until the torrent of words subsided.

Harding had expected the boy to argue back: he was used to feeding off opposition, and when it didn't come, he found it difficult to sustain his tide of anger. Anyway, he had already made up his mind to have the boy back, after that strange priest from St Anne's had rung through and spoken for him. Shelf-stackers who were honest, who didn't try to pinch the goods and would work steadily without supervision, weren't all that easy to come by, and this lad had filled the bill well for several months. Harding looked at the scrawny, penitent figure. 'I can see from the look of you that you've been ill, Joe, but you should have let someone here know. Make sure you do that, if it happens again. You can start again on Monday morning.'

Monday had seemed to Joe to last an awful long time. He reported in at seven to stack the shelves after the weekend, and was tired out by the end of his shift at three. Then he was 'offered' three hours overtime, which he took because he could see they needed him, with two others off sick. The money would come in useful, too. He had had a long talk with Father Gillespie on Sunday afternoon, and agreed that he should get himself out of the squat and into some proper accommodation as soon as he had the money to do it.

But the three extra hours were hard, even with the extra tea break old Harding told him to take at half-past four. He watched the fingers of the big electric clock creep round towards six and thought he had never seen them move so slowly. His arms felt as if they would drop off with the lifting. It was an effort even to raise the cold water from the washbasin to his face in the staff changing room.

He didn't remember until he walked out into the bright light of the car park that he hadn't got his old van. It had been vandalized outside the squat, some time last week when he was off his head on horse. When he had the money, he'd go out to the big breaker's yard and get himself a new headlamp. He turned wearily to walk the mile or so back to the squat.

'Fancy a lift, Joe? You look as if you need it!' He didn't know where the voice had come from, at first.

Then he saw the big old Vauxhall Senator, with the passenger window wound down and the weatherbeaten face of that sergeant who had come to see him at the squat smiling up at him. He hesitated a moment, then opened the back door and slid into the capacious leather seat. He had expected the car to move off then, but the sergeant came round to the other side of the car and slid heavily on to the back seat beside him. In the driver's seat, Superintendent Lambert turned his body rather stiffly, so that he could stare across the car's interior diagonally and study Joe Ashton's face.

Joe felt trapped. He should have known that nothing was for nothing, especially from the police. And yet his exhaustion made him feel that this was a comfortable trap, if trap it was. Almost anything was worthwhile, if they dropped him at the door of the squat at the end of it.

'We hoped we'd find you here,' Hook said. 'We wanted

another word with you, you see, now that you're not shooting up.' He wouldn't tell him that they had rung the store that afternoon, had found just when he would be finishing his work for the day, had come to the car park at five to six to wait for him.

And Joe Ashton was in no state to work such things out for himself. He said wearily, 'Have you found out who killed my Kate yet?' That was how he thought of her still, when he was on his own; in his fatigue, it had slipped out to strangers.

'Not yet, Joe, but we will.' Hook watched for the boy's reaction, but learned nothing from it.

Joe said dully, 'You're no nearer to finding the man who killed her, are you?'

'Yes, we are, Joe. We'll be nearer still, if you can help us. We said we'd be back, that we'd need to talk to you when you weren't high on drugs. That's why we've come now.'

'I haven't shot up for days, now. I went to see Father Gillespie.' His eyes widened as he remembered. 'It was you who told me to do that.'

Hook smiled at him. 'Yes. It was good advice, and you took it. Not many people listen to good advice.'

'He was good to me, Father was. He's helping me get back on my feet. It was he who sent me back here, to get my job back.' He looked up at the high blank wall of the rear of Sainsbury's store above him and said as if he could not quite believe it, 'I started work again today. I've been here since seven.'

'Very good, that, Joe. And I can see you're very tired. We needn't keep you here long. Then we'll drop you off at the squat. You should get out of there, you know, as soon as you can.'

He nodded. 'Father Gillespie said that.' He looked from Hook's encouraging smile to Lambert's long, watchful face in sudden alarm. 'He's not been talking to you, has he. Father Gillespie?'

'No, he hasn't, Joe. I expect he thought you'd have the good sense to tell us everything yourself.' Hook's tones were calm and persuasive, the more so to a man sunk in fatigue, feeling the comfort of the seat beneath him, having now to fight against shutting his eyes and drifting away completely.

Yet a small part of Joe's brain insisted that he must still be careful. He said slowly, 'There's nothing to tell, is there? I must have told you everything I knew when you saw me at the squat.'

'Not everything, Joe. Not much at all, really.' Hook smiled into the face grey with exhaustion. 'You weren't in any fit state to talk to anyone then, with the amount of horse you had in your veins.'

Joe Ashton gave him a small, answering, almost conspiratorial smile. 'I was high, then, wasn't I? But not now. You couldn't even have me for possession, now. It's all gone.'

'That's good. So you'll be able to talk to us about Kate.'

'What is it you want to know?'

'When did you last see Kate, Joe?'

He was vaguely aware that they'd asked him that before, when they had caught him off his head on horse in the squat. But he couldn't remember exactly what he'd said. It must have been a lie, because he couldn't have told them the truth, could he? You needed to keep a careful note of any lies you told, so that you could repeat them when necessary: it was a bit late for him to realize that now. He said uncertainly, 'It would be on the Saturday before she died, I suppose.'

Hook felt a strange mixture of elation and disappointment. He felt the delight any CID officer feels when someone is caught out in a lie; yet he knew he didn't want this stumbling, diffident boy who had struggled back from the abyss of drug addiction to be a killer. He knew that the first rule in the detection book was 'Never get involved', but he knew also that he wasn't good at that, found it impossible to observe on occasions. He looked hard into the uncertain face. 'That's not what you told us on Thursday, Joe.'

John Lambert spoke for the first time. 'You had much better tell us the truth, Joe. It's not sensible to tie yourself in knots with more lies. We might start getting suspicious.'

They were ganging up on him now. And he had made a mistake. He felt curtains of fatigue descending across his vision. It would be so much easier to tell the truth, so long as he could keep back the ultimate facts. 'When you saw me at the flat, when did I say I last saw Kate?'

Hook glanced at Lambert, then back into the boy's troubled face. 'Let's just have the real story, Joe, shall we? Before you get yourself into any more trouble.'

Joe nodded several times, with his eyes almost shut, convincing himself of what he must do rather than agreeing with Hook. I saw her on the Sunday.'

'The Sunday when she died?'

'Yes.' Joe's eyes were shut now. His face was a mask of pain, as recollection pushed into his fatigue.

'What time, Joe?'

Hook spoke very quietly, but something of his tension must have come through, because Joe opened dark blue eyes and looked at him earnestly. 'In the evening. About eight o'clock, I think. Perhaps a bit later.'

'And what happened, Joe?'

'We were going to be an item, you know, Kate and me.'

Bert Hook resisted a sudden ridiculous impulse to correct his grammar. 'Yes. You said that on Thursday, Joe. Did Kate think that, as well?'

172

'Oh yes. We weren't arguing about that. That was agreed. We were arguing about when.'

He seemed content to stop there, and Hook had to prompt him with, 'You argued then, on that last evening together.'

'Yes. But it was only about when she was coming away with me.'

'She wouldn't go immediately?'

'No. But she should have, shouldn't she? Everything would have been all right, if we'd gone straight off. Once she'd given up dealing drugs, we needed to be somewhere else, fast.'

He was right in that, thought both his hearers. Once Malcolm Flynn had reported upwards in the chain, a girl refusing to deal would have been in mortal danger. But what had this boy done to her, when she had refused to go away with him? 'But Kate didn't want to go,' Hook prompted. 'Refused to go with you, did she, that last Sunday night?'

'Yes. We – we had a row about it. Quite a bust-up, we had.' He wanted to cry at the memory, but in his exhaustion, his eyes seemed to have forgotten how to shed tears, his brain how to issue the command to weep. 'I wanted us to go away quickly, that night, if she would. She said that wasn't practical. We needed more money. Another couple of months, she said, and then we'd have the money to set up somewhere else and live a proper life. She kept saying that: "a proper life".'

'But you didn't want to wait for that.'

'No. She said – she said she'd have thousands more, in a couple of months, if I'd just be patient. I got very angry then. I couldn't bear to think of her, in bed with other men, building up this treasure chest, as she called it.'

'No, I'd have found that difficult, too, if I'd loved a girl.' Ironically enough, it seemed that Kate Wharton had

173

been planning to make swift thousands from blackmailing some person or persons, rather than through prostitution, but this sad figure before them hadn't known that. Hook asked, almost reluctantly, 'Fierce row, was it, Joe? Harsh words exchanged?'

He nodded, eyes almost shut again now. 'It went on a long time. It was dark when I left the flat.'

Hook waited for several seconds, in case a murder confession should fall out of those jaded lips. Then he pressed him: 'Came to blows, did you, in this argument?'

At the back of Joe's mind, some danger signal was suddenly activated. This is where it must stop. He couldn't possibly tell them the rest. His eyes were suddenly wide open. 'No! No, we had the most terrible row, but it didn't come to blows. I wouldn't hit her. Not my Kate, would I?'

He sounded as if he was shouting to convince himself. Hook quietly pointed out: 'We don't know, do we, Joe? We weren't there. That's why we have to ask you about these things.' He watched the boy's thin neck slump slack as a rag doll's as he nodded agreement. 'Did you kill Kate that night, Joe? Not meaning to, of course, but finding you'd killed her before you knew what you were doing? Take her body out to your van and dump it afterwards, did you?'

'No! No, I didn't kill Kate. You mustn't think that, really you mustn't.' But his face was in his hands. And at last the tears came, as he sobbed soundlessly into his fingers. They were almost a relief.

They dropped him off at the end of Sebastopol Terrace. When you lived in a squat, it wasn't sensible to have the police dropping you off at your door, even in an unmarked car. He had stuck to his story that he hadn't killed the girl, nodded dumbly and handed over the keys when Hook said that the forensic team would need to examine his van.

They watched him as he walked, reeling with fatigue,

to the door of the squat. 'I hope the silly sod didn't do it!' said Hook, his voice gruff with emotion.

Roy Cook knew now what he had to do. He went to the old wardrobe in his room, looked for a moment at the clothes which lay at the bottom of it, then pushed them carefully into the polythene bag he had brought up with him. The shirt he had only worn twice, the maroon sweater which Julie liked, the trousers he had worn as his best. It was a pity, but all of them had better go; it was the only safe way. He stuffed underpants and socks into the top of the bag, thought about his shoes, decided they would be all right with a good vigorous clean with plenty of polish. Like most people who sought to cover their tracks, he did not realize that footwear was the most revealing item of all, the one from which the police most often got significant information.

Roy looked briefly along the terrace of houses and down the deserted road to check that no one was around. Swallows swooped and rose among the trees by the stream, at the bottom of the tiny valley, but there was no human being in sight. He went out into the back garden, climbed the slope to the back of it, and built a swift wigwam of twigs over rolled-up sheets of the *Ross Gazette.*

This was the place where he always built his fires to dispose of garden refuse, and the sticks, fallen from the trees in winter, were dead and dry. The flames licked eagerly round them as the newspapers caught fire. There was but the gentlest of breezes, away from the houses, carrying the smoke away over the hill in the last of the sun. He watched with satisfaction as his wigwam fell inwards and the base of his fire was established. Then he piled other, thicker branches on top to consolidate the blaze.

Although he had worked with wood in the forest for years now, kindling a small fire of his own like this

175

still fascinated him, still gave him a primitive, caveman's pleasure. He watched the centre of his blaze glowing red now beneath the flames, felt the heat, surprisingly intense against his legs. He put the underpants and socks into the fire first, then the shirt and the sweater, placing them in the very centre, watching the smoke thicken and blacken as the flames enveloped the wool.

'What are you doing, Roy?'

He leapt like a startled deer. His concentration upon his task had been so intense, his sense of satisfaction so complete, that he had heard nothing of his visitor's arrival.

It was Julie. It could have been no one else, for she was the only one who had a key to his front door. She called out, 'I knocked, but you couldn't hear me,' and came smiling up the long, narrow garden.

She hadn't realized. Perhaps there was still time. Roy pushed the shirt with its tell-tale pattern further into the heart of the blaze, put the trousers, the last of the garments, hastily on top of the rest. But it was no good. His fire wasn't big enough, not to swallow and destroy the evidence in the few seconds he had left.

Julie was at his side in a moment, her smile turning to bafflement, and then to something much worse. 'What are you doing?' she said in a distant voice.

'Just burning a few old things.' He knew he couldn't lie effectively to her, knew that his explanation was ridiculous, but he could think of nothing else. 'I had the fire going well, and I just thought—'

'Those aren't old things.' Her voice was like ice. 'Those trousers are practically new. And that's the shirt I gave you at Christmas. What's going on, Roy?'

'Nothing, really. I just—'

'You don't burn new things. You couldn't care less about fashion, but you don't waste money on clothes. Why are you burning things that are practically new?'

He had an inspiration. 'Well, I didn't want to tell you this, but I never really fancied that shirt. I'm a bit more fashion-conscious than you thought, you see! I didn't want to hurt your feelings, though, so I thought that if I just quietly disposed of it, along with a few other—'

'You're lying, Roy. You liked that shirt, insofar as you get excited by anything you put on your back. And why burn new trousers and a good sweater, which you chose yourself?'

She stood facing him, hands moving to her hips, her joy on her arrival here dismissed as completely as if it was now weeks, not minutes, behind her. Roy could think of nothing else to say that would not make the situation worse. He turned back to the fire with his stick, turning the garments she had mentioned, pushing them further into the centre of the fire. He could hear her breathing fiercely behind him, but he would not, could not, turn to face her. The smoke rose slowly in front of him, the clothes obstinately refusing to disappear with the speed he had hoped for.

Eventually, she addressed his back, in a flat voice which frightened him more than more obvious fury. 'You were seeing Kate, weren't you?'

Still he could not turn. 'Yes, I saw her. Four or five times in the last two years, that's all.'

'You fucked her, didn't you?' The harsh word, the word she used only as a command in the extremes of their love-making, came like a bolt between his shoulders, making him wince, crippling him with his shame.

'Yes. Not the first time I saw her. But the other times, yes. I – I don't know why.'

'Good shag, was she? Better than her mother, I expect.'

He turned at last with this second brutal word, feeling her pain, wanting to stop the tide of abuse he knew would go on and on, not knowing how to do it. 'No, Julie, no one is better than you. You should know that. I'm sorry I ever went near her. We have something—'

The words of apology broke the dam, and she flung herself upon him, mouthing obscenities, tearing at the flesh of his arms with her nails, trying to scratch, even to bite, the face she had thought she loved. He hooped her in his strong arms, held her tight against him to stop her from striking at him, held her there for a moment until she was breathless, then carried her indoors as if she were a child's doll.

She was tense against him still, and he relaxed his hold upon her, but cautiously, lest she tear again at his flesh. He held her still, only letting her lean back a fraction, so that her face was still within a foot of his own anguished features. 'You bloody, bloody bastard!' she cursed. 'I lied for you! Lied for you to the police, about my own daughter. Said you'd only snatched a kiss, when I found you with her knickers torn half off and the girl screaming! Told the pigs you'd only made a pass at her, would have got you off the hook, if you hadn't blabbed it all out when you spoke to them!'

'I know, I know.' He spoke like one soothing a child, attempted cautiously to stroke her head, but she shook his great paw angrily away. 'I don't know why I had to see Kate again,' he muttered. 'I wanted to apologize, to put right what I'd done two years earlier. Then when I found she was on the game . . .'

He tailed away hopelessly, recognizing the impossibility of explaining this, and she had to complete his sentence for him. 'When you found she was on the game, you thought you'd have a quick shag! Compare mother with daughter, see if what she had between her legs was fresher!'

She was yelling the words into his face, and they were so near to the truth that he had no answer to them, no phrase he could produce to mitigate her pain and convey the measure of his regret. He pushed his mouth down on to hers, sought her tongue with his, breathed her name repeatedly into her ear, ran his hands up and down the familiar contours of her back, over the tense shoulder blades at the top, over the softer buttocks at the base.

They stood clasped like that for a long time, until her words subsided and she clung to him, answering his caresses with more urgent ones of her own, running her nails down his back until she broke the flesh, even through the thick material of his shirt. He carried her upstairs then, set her down gingerly upon his bed, stripped away her clothes and his own as she lay with eyes shut, whimpering softly, and made love to her. Gently, tenderly, at first, then with increasing fierceness, until they cried out with the raw passion of the coupling and came together as fiercely as they had ever done in happier times.

They lay for a long time entwined after their climax, minutes in which Roy wondered how safe it was to let her go, whether the woman who had spent herself so unashamedly in passion would still have the will and the strength to attack him as he lay naked beside her. He rolled away from her eventually without a word, and they lay on their backs beside each other, eyes closed, each wondering what thoughts were passing through the other's brain.

Eventually, without opening her eyes, she said in little more than a whisper, 'Why, Roy?'

'I don't know why. If I could turn the clock back, I would.'

'When? When was the first time?'

'Two years ago. Two years after she'd left your house.'

'She was on the game by then?' It was a question, not a statement.

'Yes, I think so.'

'Either she was or she wasn't. Be honest with me, at least.'

'Yes, she was on the game. I saw her walking the street,

179

looking for custom. It gave me a shock, that first time. A week later I went back. I – I felt we had unfinished business.' He used Kate's phrase, but without the bitterness with which she had flung it at him. 'I'd been brutal when she was at home, tried to force myself upon her. I wanted to try to put that right.'

'As if you could ever put something like that right. Oh, you fool, you great, lumbering fool, Roy Cook!'

For the first time, he heard affection beneath the exasperation. 'Kate wouldn't speak to me, not that first time. But I apologized, tried to put things right.'

'And then the second time, you told her that now she was charging for it, you'd buy a bit. That a tom wasn't allowed to discriminate among her clients.'

Again she was so near to the truth that he had no words to answer. 'Something like that, yes.'

'How many times, Roy?'

He wondered whether to lie, found that he no longer wanted to. 'Four, five. Maybe six. Spread over the last two years.'

'To spice up what you were getting from me, was it? God, you must have thought I was such a fool!'

He wondered for a moment whether she was preparing herself to spring at him again. But whatever the racing tensions of her mind, her body remained perfectly relaxed beside him. 'It was me who was the fool,' he said, 'not appreciating what I'd got!' He allowed his hand to steal tenderly over hers, wondering if it would be flung angrily aside.

'Did she threaten to tell me?'

He was a long time before he replied, as he tried to analyse the oblique words of Kate Wharton at their last meeting. 'No. But I was afraid she might. I realized what I'd got with you, what a fool I'd be to risk damage to it.'

'You were burning the clothes you wore to visit Kate, weren't you?'

'Yes. The last time. It's silly, I'm sure they couldn't connect me with her, but I wanted to be rid of them.'

He didn't dare to move, because he feared to fracture the bond of intimacy that held between them, despite what he had done, despite her questioning. But when the silence had stretched through two long minutes, he said, 'I'm going to get us a cup of tea, now,' and levered himself clumsily off the bed.

Julie Wharton lay quiet for minutes on end after he had gone, listening to Roy Cook's movements in the kitchen of his small, quiet house. When she finally opened her eyes, she felt she was taking stock of the rest of her life.

She turned on to her side, studied the fresh green leaves of the trees beyond the rectangle of window. As she watched, a thin funnel of smoke drifted slowly across the motionless trees, reminding her of the one question she had not dared to ask.

Had Roy been burning the clothes he wore to kill her daughter?

Seventeen

In the incident room at Ross Golf Club, early on Tuesday morning, DI Rushton sat with Superintendent Lambert and DS Hook. They were the only three people in the big temporary building, exchanging notes at the beginning of the day, bringing each other up to date on the information produced and checked by the rest of the thirty-man team and the forensic laboratories.

'What about the cars?' said Lambert. The vehicles belonging to people who had even a peripheral connection with the crime were being checked for any traces of the dead girl's body or clothes, but Chris Rushton knew just which ones his chief was most interested in.

'Negative, I'm afraid,' he said, flicking up the relevant page on his computer. 'Roy Cook has an old Granada hatchback. It was cleaned comprehensively by him, inside and out, on the day after the murder was discovered. That's his story, at any rate.' DI Rushton, who had not confronted any of the leading suspects, naturally inclined towards the man with a previous record of violence towards women as his killer.

Bert Hook put in: 'He didn't strike me as a car cleaner, Roy Cook. Not a man to be interested in showing his vehicle off to the neighbours on a Sunday morning in middle-class suburbia.'

Rushton nodded. 'According to what he told our uniformed boys, he was intending to take Julie Wharton away for the weekend. The car was in a mess, he said, and he cleaned it thoroughly in readiness for a dirty weekend on the night of Tuesday 8th May.'

Lambert raised his eyebrows. Neither Cook nor the dead girl's mother had said anything about going away. 'Which weekend was this?'

'The one after the murder. They didn't go, of course, once Kate Wharton had been murdered. It's obvious enough that they wouldn't. But there is no hotel booking anywhere to confirm the story. For what it's worth, Julie Wharton supports her man: she says they were planning a weekend away. Cook said they were intending to just drive off on Friday if the weather was nice and book accommodation where they fancied it.'

'You'd be able to do that in early May, I suppose,' said Lambert reluctantly.

'Nothing from Julie Wharton's Citroën Saxa. It hadn't been cleaned recently, and there were no traces of anything suspicious. And nothing from Malcolm Flynn's BMW. Plenty of traces of Class A drugs, as you might expect, but nothing which would suggest a body had been carried. We hadn't expected anything useful, of course: if this death is drugs-related, it's highly unlikely that Flynn would have killed the girl himself.'

'Anything from Richard Ellacott's vehicle?' This was Bert Hook, who, having been brought up in a Barnardo's home and been patronized in his time by many a man such as Ellacott, always found it satisfying to find a murderer among their number. Besides, Ellacott was a golfer, a captain of a club no less, and Bert's love-hate relationship with the game still inclined him to suspect villainy amongst its practitioners.

Rushton was already shaking his head. 'Ellacott had his Mercedes booked in for a full service on Monday of last week – the day the body was discovered, and the morning after it was dumped. The garage offers a valeting service, and the car's exterior was thoroughly washed and its interior was valeted before he collected it. Apparently he always has these things done with the full service, once a year.'

Lambert said, 'It's hellish convenient for him, on the day after the body was dumped.'

'We checked with the garage: Ellacott takes the car in at about this time every year for a full service, MOT and valeting. It would be a very convenient happening for a murderer, as you say, but the timing seems genuine.'

'What about Joe Ashton's old van? Don't tell me that's been in for a valet service!'

Rushton smiled grimly. 'No. But the interior is surprisingly clean. It's fourteen years old but he's only had it for the last few months, and it's as clean as a new pin inside.'

'Suspiciously so?'

Rushton shrugged. 'The lad says he's always kept it clean. Forensic say that may very well be the truth: they couldn't find any signs of neglect followed by a violent spring-clean. They did find a few fibres from the sweater Kate Wharton was wearing when she died.'

Rushton had a habit of delivering his most dramatic snippets very casually. It was Bert Hook who said sharply, 'Where?'

'On the front passenger seat, I'm afraid. They were caught on a frayed bit of piping on the back of the seat.'

Where a girlfriend might often have sat when she was alive, then. Fibres from the clothing of a corpse would almost certainly have been somewhere in the carrying space of the van, or on the rear doors, through which the body would probably have been thrust and extracted in some haste. Bert Hook sighed. In a CID man, it should have been a sigh of professional disappointment or frustration. This one sounded suspiciously like relief.

'Has Malcolm Flynn volunteered anything useful?' Rushton asked. 'To me, this killing still seems likely to be drugs-related. Kate Wharton refused to go on dealing for Flynn on Monday night, and died the following Sunday. The timing is exactly right for them to have brought in a contract killer.'

Lambert nodded grimly. 'I agree. The Drugs Squad have had a go at Flynn on this, as well as me. He's admitted that he reported to his superior on the Tuesday after that Monday night meeting that Kate Wharton was refusing to continue as a pusher. But he's stuck to his story throughout – that he knows nothing beyond that point, that he didn't kill her himself and has no idea whether the organization regarded her defection as serious enough to warrant her elimination. I don't think we're going to get any more out of him, for the simple reason that he's probably telling the truth. He certainly wouldn't be called upon to kill the girl himself, and once he'd passed the information upwards, the situation would be assessed and dealt with by someone much further up the hierarchy.'

'Keith Sugden?' Rushton mentioned the name of the biggest drugs-baron in the Midlands, who lived in a large house by the Severn, with wonderful original furniture and décor from the Arts and Crafts movement of William Morris and his followers. Sugden was a man they had never been able to bring to court, despite the expenditure over the last decade of huge police resources.

Lambert shrugged. 'It could have been. Or someone just below him in the pecking order. The probability is that we shall never know. At the moment, we don't even know for certain that this death was drugs-related.'

Bert Hook said slowly, almost reluctantly, 'That's what

I've been wondering about. Kate Wharton was well down the hierarchy. Would the defection of a simple pusher warrant a murder?'

Lambert knew the way Bert's mind worked. He didn't want to face the fact that Joe Ashton was their likeliest suspect, wished more than anything that this death might be the result of an order from a drugs baron, even if that meant they might never secure an arrest. 'Perhaps not,' he said sharply. 'But we don't know how much Kate Wharton knew about the organization. She might have found out more about the men higher up the ranks than was good for her. Prostitutes have all sorts of clients; a lot of them know more about what's going on in some parts of the criminal world than coppers.'

The three men stared glumly at the computers and the phones and the accumulated detritus of the investigation, contemplating that old, obvious frustration: in a murder investigation, you could never question the central figure, the victim, to find out exactly what she had and had not known.

The thought reminded Lambert of another fact they would never be able to query with the dead girl. 'Any further information come in on that extra thousand pounds in Kate Wharton's bank account?'

Rushton shook his head. 'Highly unlikely that she just had a good week on the game. Her takings from working the streets were paid in regularly and were always about the same amount. There's no evidence of a sugar daddy and Joe Ashton claims to know nothing about it. Certainly he wouldn't have had the funds to provide her with a thousand pounds unless he'd been nicking property or dealing drugs, and there's no evidence that he did either. He was keeping his nose clean, working at Sainsbury's, and insists that he was only upset that he couldn't get Kate Wharton to go away with him.'

'Could it have been an extra payment for her drugs dealing?' said Hook.

'That's always possible, but it seems unlikely, since she was planning to give up pushing altogether, and did so less than a month later. Blackmail of some kind is the likeliest explanation. Toms are always in a position to bring pressure to bear on clients, but it's a dangerous game.'

As it may well have proved in this case. Lambert pursued this: 'Two of our suspects, at least, are candidates. Roy Cook wouldn't have wanted her to tell her mother that he'd been seeing her. It might even have seemed something like justice for the girl, after he'd attempted to rape her in her mother's house.'

'And Richard Ellacott,' said Hook grimly. 'He wouldn't have wanted his invalid wife to find out he had a regular arrangement with a prostitute. Still less his cronies at the golf club, if you ask me.'

'But we can't pin that payment down,' Rushton pointed out. 'It could still be from her drug supplier, an advance payment for services which she failed to deliver, and paid the ultimate price. They don't hold back when anyone attempts to double-cross them, those people.'

'Time for coffee,' said Lambert abruptly, and led the way across the car park and into the clubhouse.

The steward served them assiduously in the deserted lounge. The murder on the Ross course had already given him a certain standing, and he was anxious to keep himself up to date with the case, knowing that a succession of members would be anxious for the latest news as they came to the bar during the day. He came back into the room when they had almost finished their coffee. 'Made an arrest yet, Mr Lambert?' he said as he set a fresh coffee-jug before them.

'Our enquiries are proceeding satisfactorily. We expect

developments before too long,' intoned Lambert magisterially.

His two companions grinned, but the steward seemed unaware of any irony in the delivery of these professional clichés. He grinned confidentially. 'Put the wind up a few of our golfers, I can tell you, when they found they were being questioned about their whereabouts on that night!'

'I can imagine,' said Lambert sourly. 'Just the routine of a murder investigation. They weren't the only ones.' He wished the man would go away and leave them in peace with the second coffee-jug.

But the steward lingered. 'No, I heard you were questioning people at all the golf clubs in the area. Even gave Mr Ellacott from Oldford Golf Club a grilling, I hear.' The steward grinned happily at this evidence of the golfing grapevine among golf club employees.

Lambert glanced up at him sharply from his armchair. 'He thought he could save us a bit of time by giving us his thoughts about his members. Mr Ellacott's the Captain at Oldford this year.'

The steward smirked, anxious to show how much he was in touch with golf club affairs. 'Yes, I know. Nice chap, Mr Ellacott. He made a good speech when he was up here with their C team a couple of weeks ago. Very complimentary about the meal we served, he was.'

'I'm sure he was, George. But at the moment—'

Rushton's mobile phone shrilled suddenly in his pocket, and he took it away to the far corner of the big lounge, speaking animatedly into the mouthpiece while the steward and his two colleagues watched him and speculated. The Detective Inspector's urgent look as he switched off the phone brought his two colleagues swiftly out of the clubhouse with him, leaving the disappointed George to clear away the coffee cups.

'That was the Drugs Squad Superintendent. One of

his undercover men has just reported in. Minton was
seen in Ross-on-Wye on the Sunday when Kate Wharton
was killed.'

The name rang like an alarm-bell in their ears. Derek
Minton was a contract killer. The one usually used by
Keith Sugden's drugs syndicate.

John Lambert found the bungalow empty when he popped
home for lunch. He had forgotten that Christine was
working again, that this was one of the days when she
lunched at the school where she taught for half of the
week. It seemed to emphasize the bleakness of his own
impending retirement, that event he was still refusing to
think about as he wrestled with the complexities of the
Kate Wharton murder.

He made himself a cheese sandwich and sat staring
unseeingly at a lunch-time financial programme on BBC 2
that he had never seen before. An item on pensions said that
with life expectancy continually increasing, people should
plan in the expectation of living well into their eighties. It
did not seem at that moment a pleasant prospect.

He wandered into the garden with a mug of tea in his
hand. The roses were coming on well, with new growth
evident even since yesterday; the climbing rose 'Breath of
Life', enjoying the warmth of the south-west facing brick
wall, was already full of buds. Its name danced in front of
him on its plastic tag like a taunt from nature. The peonies
held fat buds above their crimson spring foliage, waiting
to burst into luxuriant flower. The grass was growing
extravagantly after steady rain through the night, needing
another cut scarcely three days after its last one. In the wood
beyond the garden, beeches were parading the impossibly
fresh green of their new leaves. All around him was new,
abundant life.

He wandered through his own neat patch of this idyllic

scene, forcing himself to rejoice conventionally in the abundance of growth around him, in the magical renewal of the season. He set down his mug for a moment, removed a couple of weeds from beneath the roses, wrenched the first young convolvulus from its attempt to twine itself round the pyracantha. When he picked up his mug of hot tea, it left a circle of yellowed grass which it had burnt upon the lawn.

He stared at it for a moment, almost glad of this tiny patch of death amongst the profusion of growth. That small round of grass was dead. The healthy grass around it would expand and cover the gap, but it would take time. About three months: the time until his retirement.

He had forgotten the television. There was an old black and white film on now, with Robert Mitchum. It had never been very good, even forty years ago, when it had been as new as the growth beyond the wide window of the sitting room. Was this how the retired spent their days, regurgitating experiences which had been second-class when they were young, gilding the mediocre with the nostalgia of recollection?

He switched the television set off with a violence he could never recall before.

There would be better things to watch, he told himself unconvincingly. He would enjoy the cricket and the golf he had never had the time to watch before. Meanwhile, he still had three months of useful life left, and there was a murderer at large somewhere, a murderer it was his duty to trap. He scribbled a message for Christine, informing her that he would very likely be late home, that the investigation was developing, so that he couldn't say with any certainty when he would return.

There was no need for it. His wife had grown used over thirty years and more to the exigencies of his job. But writing the message seemed a defiant gesture, an assertion that he still had work to do. As he finished it, his phone rang to confirm just that.

Rushton could not keep the excitement out of his voice. 'They've spotted Minton in Edgbaston.' Contract killing was a lucrative occupation, enabling its practitioner to live in an ivy-walled house in a quiet close of one of the country's plushest suburbs. 'They want to know what action they should take.'

John Lambert hesitated for no more than a second. 'Tell them to pull him in. I'll be up there within ninety minutes to interview him myself.'

Eighteen

Joe Ashton was relieved when his van was returned to him by the police. The uniformed officers made no comment when he collected it, but the CID men seemed to have accepted his story that he had always kept the interior of the vehicle very clean. At any rate, they hadn't come back to him with more questions about it.

The store had had deliveries of tinned foods and of Sainsbury's own labels on that Tuesday morning, and Joe was kept busy replenishing the shelves of the supermarket and making a series of journeys to the storerooms at the rear of the building. The trouble with this job, he decided, was that it left you too much time to think. The physical labour was steady and demanding, but once you had mastered the limited information about what went where and in what quantities, there were few demands on the brain.

And Joe's brain needed to be fully stretched. When it wasn't, it kept coming back to Kate. He was coming to terms with her death now, though he grieved for her with a painful, grinding sorrow in the early part of the day, when the low sun stole unbidden through the uncurtained windows of the squat and reawakened him each morning to the realization that she was gone.

But what he didn't want to think about was that last, fierce argument they had endured. The pain of it did not become less sharp with the passing days. The thought of their last meeting ending like that would be with him for ever, even if he was never forced to reveal the full horror of what had happened.

The police seemed to accept his latest version of it, that he and Kate had had a furious row because she refused to come away with him and leave Gloucester and its memories behind. He hadn't told them about the blows, about the red mist of fury she had brought to him when she had told him she must go on extracting money from men. They mustn't ever know about the violence of those final minutes.

Joe Ashton went on methodically replacing the tins of baked beans.

Derek Minton did not look like a professional killer. It was true that he was wiry and thin-faced, with cold blue eyes and the mean mouth and thin lips one might have expected in a man who dealt in passionless violence. But he was also well dressed, in a grey suit more expensive than the one Lambert wore, with a discreet maroon silk tie laced with silver motifs and elegant slip-on Barker shoes. He had neatly styled brown hair and hands which were clean and strong-fingered enough to have been a pianist's. His nails were spotless, and the watch upon his wrist was probably a Rolex.

He put away his book unhurriedly as Lambert came into the interview room and sat down opposite him. The two studied each other wordlessly for three or four seconds, which seemed to the young PC who had come into the room with Lambert to stretch much longer.

Then Minton said calmly, 'I could have you for wrongful arrest, you know, if I chose.'

'But you won't. Your sort doesn't want publicity. You won't go into a court until we eventually put you into the dock.'

'Which will be never. Because I'm an innocent citizen.'

Lambert smiled his contempt for that thought. 'Do you want a lawyer?'

'Are you charging me with anything?'

'That remains to be seen. At this point, no.'

'Then I don't want a lawyer. I don't want anything which will enable you to prolong this farce for longer than is necessary.'

'You're a killer, Minton. It's how you make a living.'

'Prove it.'

Lambert thought of mentioning two killings in Birmingham's gangland that they were certain Minton had committed. But they hadn't been able to prove it, hadn't been able to provide the witnesses to go into court and put this suave and confident man away for life. So he said instead, 'You were seen in Ross-on-Wye on Sunday the sixth of May.'

'Nice part of the country. Nice time of the year. Enjoyed the trip.'

'On that day, a twenty-two-year-old girl named Kate Wharton was strangled.'

'Pity. The world needs more twenty-two-year-old girls.'

'This one was a hard-drugs pusher. She worked for an organization which regularly makes use of your services. Six days earlier, she had told her supplier that she intended to give up pushing.'

'Naughty little tart, wasn't she? Some people would say she had it coming to her. Not me, of course.'

'How did you know she was on the game?'

For a moment, he looked disconcerted by this minor mistake. In the trade of killing, you planned carefully and didn't even allow yourself minor mistakes. Then he smiled. 'I did not mean the word literally when I spoke, Superintendent. If you're now telling me that the girl was indeed on the game, that is no more than a happy semantic coincidence. Interesting things, semantics.'

'Why were you in Ross nine days ago?'

'I'm not sure I have to tell you that. But as I always like to co-operate with the police, let's say I was visiting friends.'

'And it's just a coincidence that Kate Wharton was killed that night.'

'Exactly. A most unhappy one. A more vindictive man than me might say she had it coming to her, being a prostitute and dealing in drugs. Such a person might even say that the world was well rid of such an occupant. But I don't care to strike moral attitudes.'

'Of course you don't.' Lambert leaned forward towards the calm face with the sardonic smile. 'You were there to kill the girl, Minton. That was no pleasure trip.'

Derek Minton didn't even trouble to deny it. He merely shrugged his elegant shoulders beneath the expensive worsted. He didn't need to defend himself. They'd nothing to go on. He'd been pulled in for questioning often enough before, had been much nearer to a murder charge than this. Did they expect him to be frightened like some kid who'd pinched a wallet?

Minton pulled out a slim gold cigarette case, flicked it open, offered it across the desk to his would-be inquisitor. Lambert waved it away and said, 'No smoking in here.'

Minton raised an eyebrow, then snapped the gold case shut and put it away with a smile. The incident had ruffled the questioner more than the questioned: he was glad he had conducted this little charade from a previous era. 'How did this girl die?' he asked casually.

'You know that. She was garrotted with a cord. Taken from behind and killed within seconds.'

'Efficient, then. But not a method I would have chosen.'

That was true enough; it had worried Lambert on the journey up the M5. The killings they knew Minton had committed but could not pin on him were all with the bullet, swift and effective, usually through the head from point-blank range. 'You agree you have a method, then?'

195

Minton wasn't ruffled. 'Not at all. I merely quote the method I was supposed to have used when you concocted your previous fictions.'

'A professional like you is adaptable. The cord was the right method for this situation. When you pick up a tom on the streets and she slides willingly into your car, you don't want anything as noisy as a bullet.'

Minton studied the long, lined face and the intense grey eyes for a moment. This was so near to what he had planned that he did not want to give anything away. He said slowly, without dropping his eyes from Lambert's, 'I bow to your superior knowledge, Superintendent.'

'Who called you down there to kill the girl, Minton?'

Derek Minton smiled. For a moment, he said nothing: he was enjoying this, but he knew that it was a dangerous enjoyment. Pleasure could catch you off your guard more easily than any other feeling. He had killed nine people now, with an increasing price for each death as his reputation for anonymous efficiency grew. In his judgement, he had come quite near to being charged on two occasions. The police had probably thought there were the makings of a case each time, but the Crown Prosecution Service had been afraid to take it on: good old CPS, scourge of petty criminals and friend of the big boys!

The fuzz weren't going to get him on this one, weren't going to come anywhere near to a charge. He knew that, and they must know it as well, by now. He repeated with a bland smile, 'I was visiting friends. Nice river, the Wye.'

Lambert forced himself into an answering smile. He wouldn't let the man see the frustration and revulsion which boiled within him. He pushed back his seat and stood up. 'If you did it, we'll be back for you. You're living on borrowed time, Mr Minton.'

Derek Minton raised an imaginary glass to him as he left.

Lambert gave curt orders for Minton's release to the custody sergeant. He hadn't expected anything from the interview. He told himself that as he drove more slowly back down the M5, attempting to calm himself. He had known he had nothing beyond a sighting in Ross on the sixth of May to throw at Minton, had known that someone as experienced as this would not be intimidated, would offer him nothing in the way of emotional weakness. But he had hoped with his experience to be able to size up whether the man had done the killing, irrespective of whether they could bring him to book for it.

He spent the time on the M5 and the M50 wondering whether Minton's confidence had been derived from the fact that he had not committed this particular crime, or whether it was a professional carapace, a bland contempt for a system which could not prove his guilt.

Richard Ellacott drew out the two thousand pounds from the NatWest Bank in Ross. No one behind the counter at the bank seemed to turn a hair, for they were used to his firm dealing in large sums. Even the fact that he drew the money in cash raised no eyebrows: he was an accountant, wasn't he, and accountants had ways and means of doing business which avoided tax. Probably he was just having some extensive work done in his home and paying for it in cash; Richard tried to create that impression.

It was a load off his mind to get back to the Mercedes and lock the money away in the glove compartment. He had expected to attract more attention when withdrawing that amount in cash.

His relief did not last long. He would have to deliver the money to his blackmailer on Thursday. And then he would be faced again with the fear that the anonymous woman might come back for more, the waiting for that nightmare phone call that would again set his ordered world spinning out of control.

That blank voice had said that this would be the final demand, but there was nothing he could reclaim to guarantee that – no photographic negatives or documents which he could bargain for and take back. This was simply knowledge: the knowledge that he had visited a prostitute, not once but regularly over a long period, whilst he pretended to be a pillar of society and a diligent attendant upon his invalid wife.

But the blackmailer had assured him that this doubly big demand for two thousand pounds would be a final, one-off payment. All might yet be well, if you could trust a blackmailer to keep her word.

Like many a weak man before him, Richard Ellacott took refuge in a sickly, unrealistic hope.

Julie Wharton had a busy day in the office at Cheltenham. There were queries from the junior clerical staff, a request from the senior partner to sit in on a meeting in the afternoon and take notes.

It was as well she was kept busy, for each time she had a moment to herself her mind revived the vivid picture of Roy Cook burning his new clothes at the end of his deserted garden. She knew she had let her physical desire for him obscure the issue. That other Julie, the one she scarcely acknowledged when she moved about the office in her trim skirt and demure blouse, had blinded her brain to the issue, whilst she sated her desire for Roy's powerful body.

In the cold light of day, in the practical environment of work, the question gnawed at her: would Roy have been burning those clothes unless they bound him in some way to Kate's death? Unless Julie had arrived unexpectedly at his isolated house, the evidence, if that was what it was, would have been destroyed for ever, without anyone but

Roy knowing about it. As it was, the evidence was gone, but she was a witness to its destruction.

She ought to go to the police, ought to let them take up the questioning, to make Roy give an account of himself, in a way she would never be able to do. But he had a record: they would surely seize upon what he had done to his clothes to pin the responsibility for Kate's death upon him, wouldn't they? And she couldn't betray him like that, couldn't simply walk into the police station and grass on him, without even telling Roy what she proposed to do.

It would be different if the police came to her, if that insistent Lambert and his deceptively observant sergeant came and wormed it out of her. Roy would accept that – hadn't they got far more out of him than he had intended to give them? But throughout her busy day, there came no phone call from the quietly insistent Hook to arrange another meeting with the CID men.

She would have to confront Roy herself. And this time she would do it on her own territory. And she wouldn't allow herself to be diverted by other considerations.

Roy came to her house at half-past six that evening, as they had arranged that he would. She had a meal ready and the table set; they sat primly on opposite sides of it in the bay of her neat dining room, whilst the sun disappeared round the corner of the house as it moved to the west. They exchanged notes about their day, each conscious of what lay between them, each unwilling to raise it. Julie brought coffee to the table at the end of the meal, ignoring Roy's suggestion that they take it away from the table to sit more comfortably in armchairs, as they usually did.

She introduced the subject without preamble, moving in directly to the core of it as he might have done himself. 'Why did you burn those clothes, Roy? You said you hadn't seen Kate for days before she died.'

He didn't refuse to talk about it, as she had thought he

199

might. Rather it was as if he had been waiting for her to speak. 'I just felt there might be something of Kate upon them, that's all. With my record, that might have been all they needed, especially when I'd denied seeing her at all at first.'

Julie thrust aside the image of Kate in his arms, pressed tight against him, leaving evidence of herself on his trousers, on his sweater, on the shirt she had bought for him herself. 'But if you hadn't seen her for several days before she was killed, you had nothing to fear.'

'No. And I'd no need to burn them. I could have had them cleaned, couldn't I? But I wasn't acting rationally. I just wanted to destroy anything that might connect me with Kate, and the fire seemed the most final solution.'

It was that all right, she thought. And if I hadn't come upon you doing it, no one would have been any the wiser. Roy was no actor. He had delivered these last words to her like a prepared statement, one he had been thinking about during the day. No wonder he had been unable to deceive the police. Something struck her now with the force of a revelation. 'You saw her later than you said, didn't you?'

He looked directly at her for the first time since this had started, and there was fear in his dark eyes. He nodded.

'When?'

'On the Sunday. In the afternoon.'

She looked down, saw knuckles white with tension on the table, realized with a shock that they were her own. 'So you went round there and shagged my daughter, then came to me in the evening.' The harshness of the obscenity was a release, a tiny safety valve for the pressure she felt would burst her body.

'No. We didn't – we didn't do that. She'd said she was planning to go away, to make a fresh start somewhere else with Joe. That was her boyfriend.'

'So you went round there for a final fuck.' She tried to put all her anger into the alliteration.

'No. We didn't – didn't make love. I told you. She wouldn't.'

What a great fool he was, she thought in the midst of her rage. He was even admitting that it was only Kate's refusal that had prevented it happening. It made him defenceless, this stumbling, unwilling honesty. It was like hitting a man who would not raise his hands. She said dully, 'You killed Kate, didn't you? That's why you were burning your clothes!'

'No. I wanted her to stay, and she wouldn't. She held me, kissed me goodbye, that was all. I felt the smell of her was on those clothes.'

And probably it was, she thought. And other things as well, like fibres. And other, more personal things, if he was not telling the truth, if he had done more with her daughter on that last day than he said.

He came round the table and put his hands on her shoulders, but she shook him angrily away. She would not let him clasp her tonight, would not let him confuse her mind with passion, as he had done at his own house. She sent him back there to sleep alone, hoping he would have the disturbed night she knew lay ahead of her.

At three o'clock the next morning sleep had still not come to Julie Wharton. She looked at her bedside clock and wondered for the twentieth time whether the man with whom she was planning to spend the rest of her life had killed her only child.

Nineteen

L ambert stared at the cereal packet, wondering what it was that nagged at the fringes of his mind, trying to isolate the one fact among a thousand which had struck a jarring note. The thought had come to him again during the night that he had missed something, some connection he should have made.

Then an urgent phone call from DI Rushton sent Lambert leaping from the breakfast table, leaving his cereals, his wife and his house like an eager young constable.

Bert Hook was already there when he got to the incident room, standing grim-faced at the shoulder of Chris Rushton as the younger man sat at his computer. The latter glanced round to make sure they were unobserved; he ran his life strictly by the book, and it worried him when other people did not do the same. He knew Bert Hook was as straight as they came, that he had only done what any efficient detective would have done, that all CID men bent the rules a little from time to time, but he was nonetheless uneasy when confronted directly with the results of this.

But those results were in this case spectacular. Bert Hook's habit of collecting samples from any leading suspect for DNA testing were not officially allowed: unless the subjects volunteered, you were supposed to make an arrest before you took DNA samples and compared them with evidence collected at the scene of a crime. What Hook's initiative had now thrown up for them could not be produced as evidence in court. But that scarcely mattered: once they had their man under lock and key, other, more official DNA samples could be taken. Those would be the ones quoted in any subsequent court case.

Meanwhile, Rushton's information was terse and to the point. 'Forensic have come up with a match,' he said. 'The skin samples taken from under Kate Wharton's nails match up with one of the hair samples DS Hook sent in for analysis.'

'I gathered that when you rang me at home!' said Lambert impatiently. 'We'll go straight out and get him. Which one is it?'

He felt he already knew the answer an instant before the DI said brusquely, 'Joe Ashton.'

Richard Ellacott was waiting by the phone in his study when it rang. He snatched it up on the first ring.

The voice said in an even, slightly muffled tone, 'You've got the money?'

For a moment, it sounded more like a statement than a question in his fearful ears, and he had the nightmare vision of being watched as he went into the bank, of being observed like a fly in a web as he struggled to free himself. Then the words were repeated and he answered dully, 'Yes, I've got it.'

'Tomorrow night, then.'

'All right. Where exactly?'

Tracey Boyd put her mouth a little nearer to the tights she had wrapped round the mouthpiece and said softly, 'The road where you picked up Kate, the first time.'

This mysterious, anonymous voice seemed to know everything about him. He licked his lips. 'All right. What do—'

'Have the cash in a plastic bag. And don't be silly enough to let anyone else know what you're doing.'

'No. I won't do that. But you did say this was the final demand you'd make on me. I don't want—'

'Of course. The one and only demand. Two thousand. Cheap, for keeping quiet about what I know.'

'Just so long as it's understood that—'

But the phone had gone dead. Richard stared at it dumbly for a few moments after he had put it down. As he walked slowly into the hall, his wife's frail voice from above asked him who had rung.

'Wrong number, dear,' he said cheerfully. 'It took me a little time to convince them that they'd got the wrong person, that's all.'

Joe Ashton was not at the squat. There was no sign of him or his treasured van. But they found that tell-tale vehicle parked outside the high stone walls of St Anne's House in Gloucester.

Father Jason Gillespie appeared as if by some psychic agency on the top step of the building as they approached. He was plainly out to defend this particular resident. He stood small and foursquare as they approached, with his legs a little apart, like the bare-fisted pugilists who had fought when this nineteenth-century building was in its heyday. Grey-haired and with his face prematurely lined, he should have been a ridiculous figure as he set himself against the forces of the law, but his determination gave him a kind of dignity.

The two CID men stopped respectfully before him. Lambert's eyes were nearly level with the priest's, though he stood two steps below him, as Gillespie said, 'He's a guest here, gentlemen. I know this isn't a church, but I try to afford my guests a form of sanctuary.'

It was Bert Hook who put him straight. 'We can't accept that, I'm afraid, Father. It's gone beyond that. Joe Ashton has lied to us about his part in a murder. We have to

204

speak to him. He'll get justice: we can't promise any more than that.'

The priest looked for a moment as if he would resist them. Then he saw that Hook's face looked even more troubled than his own and stood wordlessly aside to let them into the hall. He said from behind them, 'You'll find him in the dormitory, I expect. He's not due at work until twelve, today. You can take him into my office if you need privacy.'

The priest came to the bottom of the stairs as Hook plodded heavily after his chief and called at the broad retreating back, 'If you arrest him, I'd like to come to the station with him. He hasn't anyone else.' Bert paused in his stride for a moment, looked down at Gillespie with a sympathetic smile, and nodded.

Joe Ashton was not in fact in the dormitory, but in the big bathroom ten yards down the landing, cleaning the second of a row of four washbasins. He looked up in surprise as they came into the room. Surprise was followed by the look Bert Hook least wanted to see, one of apprehension moving towards panic.

'We need words with you, Joe Ashton,' Lambert told him. 'Let's have you in Father Gillespie's room, now.'

He sat behind the priest's big desk, leaving Hook to sit nearer to Ashton, only half-facing him. The youth's slim frame had scarcely touched the upright wooden chair before Lambert said, 'You lied to us about Kate Wharton, Joe. We want to know why. And this time I advise you to come up with the truth.'

'I don't know what you're talking about. I told you, I loved Kate. I want you to arrest whoever it was who—'

'Then tell us the truth, and stop buggering us about!'

There was no mistaking Lambert's fury, and Ashton quivered before it. 'What – what is it you want to know?'

Bert Hook spoke more quietly but no less urgently;

he was no more than three feet from the young man's right ear. 'Your last meeting with Kate, Joe. What really happened?'

The already frightened face seemed to turn still whiter. 'I told you. We had a terrible row. I wanted her to come away with me—'

'And she wouldn't. We've heard all that, Joe. Heard about this terrible row. Now tell us how you killed her. How you dumped the body in the back of your van and hid it in that ditch on the golf course.' Lambert's voice was harsh with frustration, as he reversed the compassion he had felt earlier for this confused boy, who had fought back from drug addiction and then plunged himself into the nightmare world of murder.

'But I didn't! I didn't kill Kate. I never wanted to hurt her, let alone kill her.'

Hook's voice came again from his right, calm, per-suasive, even sympathetic. 'Maybe you didn't intend to kill her, Joe. If you didn't, you might get away with a manslaughter charge.'

The face which turned to Hook was a boy's face, stripped of artifice, filled only with a desperate fear. 'But I didn't kill her! We had a row, but I didn't kill her! I don't know why you should think that I would ever have—'

'She fought with you, Joe!' Lambert's harsh voice tore the boy from his despairing attempt to convince Hook. 'We know that. We know that you didn't just fling words at each other. It went beyond that. Fragments of your skin and your hair were found beneath her nails!'

Ashton's eyes, widening in horror until it seemed for a moment as if they would never shut again, turned back to Hook. 'It's true, Joe,' Bert said quietly. 'Part of the procedure when anyone dies from violence is to take samples from beneath the nails of the corpse, which are then analysed in the forensic laboratories. There were definite traces of material matching your DNA beneath Kate's nails.'

Joe didn't question where they had got the DNA sample for the match. The police to him were now omniscient. He told them dully, 'We quarrelled, like I said. We fought with each other – I didn't tell you that. But I didn't kill her.'

Hook said softly, insistently, 'You'll need to convince us of that, Joe.'

Ashton turned slowly until he stared full into the Detective Sergeant's face, as if he hoped to find sympathy here that he could not expect from the iron-faced superintendent. 'We did quarrel, the way I told you on Monday. But it was worse than I said. I called her a slag, because she wouldn't come away with me, because she wanted to go on taking money from men. And she flew at me.'

'So you fought each other. And before you realized what was happening, you'd killed her.'

'No!' His voice rose to a yell, telling them that hysteria was not far away. 'I didn't even hit her! Not really. I just tried to protect myself when she flew at me. She marked me. It's almost better now.' He pulled down the neck of his T-shirt, showing a scratch at the base of his neck that had almost gone, and then a longer, more livid laceration across his chest, which was also healing. They sensed that he had preserved these last traces of the dead girl as long as possible, the relics of a lost love.

There was a long pause before Lambert asked, 'Have you anything to add to that? Any variation to your latest version of what happened?'

He tried to keep the harshness in his voice, to invest the words with a savage irony. But the boy seemed to sense that there was a chance after all that he might be believed. He said quietly, 'No. I've told you everything I know this time.'

'And why not earlier? You say you want Kate's killer

arrested. Why not tell us the truth in the first place. If it is the truth, that is.'

'I was scared. You must see that. Scared shitless.' He glanced up like a guilty schoolboy who fears his language will bring fresh retribution. 'A druggy going with a girl on the game. I didn't think you'd look any further.'

Lambert stood up. 'We'll need a statement from you in due course. We'll expect to find you here, when we need you. If you go anywhere else, let someone know at Oldford CID.' When he met Father Gillespie on the stairs, he managed his first smile since Rushton had told him of the DNA samples. 'You don't need to come to the station, Father, not for the moment. He'll tell you what he's told us. If he adds anything more, it's your duty to get in touch with us.' He was out of the building and into the clear sunlight of the May morning before the priest could express either relief or co-operation.

Hook had driven for five minutes before his chief stated: 'If he killed her, it wasn't manslaughter, Bert. The girl was garrotted with a cord round her neck. It was a deliberate act: cold-blooded murder.'

'I know that. I was trying to get him to talk. He seemed terrified enough to confess to anything at the time.'

They went another half-mile before Lambert said, 'There were no bruises on the body. No real marks, apart from that one awful wound round the neck.'

It was an acknowledgement that the boy's story was probably true, a recognition that Hook had been right in encouraging him to give his account of that last meeting. Bert knew his chief well enough to recognize that, without it being put into words.

And for his part, John Lambert had just recognized what it was that had been irritating the edge of his mind for the last twenty-four hours.

Twenty

It was late morning when the phone call came. Richard
Ellacott hesitated for a moment before he answered,
hand poised over the instrument, wondering if it would be
the blackmailer again with a change of orders. It was almost
a relief to hear the rich Herefordshire voice of DS Hook.

The relief did not last for more than a few seconds. 'We
need to see you again. Right away.' Hook's voice was
quiet, but there was a gravity in it which set Richard's
pulse racing.

'All right. I was just about to go over to the golf club
at Oldford. I could see you there after lunch, if you like.
Shall we say two o'clock?'

'It's more urgent than that. And we don't think Oldford
Golf Club is the appropriate place, this time. Stay where
you are, please, Mr Ellacott. We'll be round at your house
in quarter of an hour.'

Richard put the phone down and tried to think. But now,
when he most needed it, his brain would not work for him.
He could not think what preparations he should be making
for this latest meeting, could not rehearse the answers to
questions he might be asked, because his mind would not
frame the questions.

He went heavily upstairs to his wife's bedroom, sought
refuge in the physical actions of tidying the room and
straightening the bed where she lay. The multiple schlerosis
was in one of the phases where it made the rapid and

J. M. Gregson

debilitating progress which alarmed them both. Eileen had
fallen yesterday, and they had agreed that she should stay
in bed today until the late afternoon or evening.

She had endured a bad night, and she lay still and quiet
beneath the blankets. She had been trying to do the *Times*
crossword, but had dropped the paper beside the bed and
been too exhausted to retrieve it. Richard picked it up,
folded it neatly, and put it back upon the bedside table.
He saw with a pang that she had been able to insert only
three answers in the puzzle.

She watched his every movement about the room, her
febrile eyes glittering unnaturally large in the small white
face. He opened the window wide, trying not to notice the
stale smell of ill health in the room. He told her it was a
bright day outside, but fresher, less warm than the previous
one – as if the coolness were somehow a compensation for
her being unable to go out into the air today.

The small statements about their life together which
normally dropped from him automatically would not come
easily now. He wanted to make bigger statements: to tell
her that he loved her; to recall their life before her illness
as the idealized partnership it had never been; to tell her
that whatever he had done, he loved her more, not less,
than in those earlier years. Yet how could he embark on
such things and yet pretend that everything was normal,
that nothing had happened to provoke such declarations?

'Those CID chaps are coming to see me again, Eileen.
Still trying to clear up a few loose ends, I expect, though
I can't think any of our members at Oldford would have
been involved in the murder of that girl. They said they'd
see me at the golf club, but I said I'd rather they came
here, where there would be a little more privacy.'

He wondered as he went back down the stairs why he
had produced that pointless lie for her.

He was glad to see as the policemen pulled into the

210

drive that they hadn't come in one of those garish police cars and advertised their visit to the neighbours. They were in the Superintendent's big old Vauxhall Senator: a nice enough car in its day, but Richard wondered why he didn't have something more modern. Still, the veteran detective with his quiet manner, who seemed all the time to see a little beyond the answers he was given, was plainly his own man.

Richard took them into his study, where he had set two armchairs out ready for them. He sat on his swivel chair and swung it round to face them. He felt at home here, with the framed confirmation of his qualification as a chartered accountant and his picture of the Swilken Bridge at St Andrews on the wall, and the modest collection of golfing trophies he had acquired over the years on the shelves. 'We'll be private enough in here,' he remarked. 'And we won't be disturbed: my wife had a fall yesterday and is staying in bed today.'

'I'm sorry about that,' said Lambert. It was no more than formal politeness, and yet he found that he meant it. The frail woman upstairs was suffering quite enough without what he now had to bring to her.

Richard found he had to fill the pause which followed, as these two experienced men studied his face. 'I've kept my ear to the ground at the club, as you asked me to, but I haven't come up with anything useful. I must say that I shall be surprised if any of our members at Oldford have any connection with the dumping of this girl's body on the course at Ross-on-Wye.'

There was no need for a cat-and-mouse game here, and Lambert found even the notion of one distasteful. He said quietly, 'Mr Ellacott, we know how you killed her, and we think we know why. I'd be interested to hear your version of how it happened.'

Richard tried hard to simulate astonishment and outrage.

211

'I hope you're joking, Superintendent Lambert! Though a joke in such bad taste should surely not go unreported.'

But he felt now that he had known all along that this was inevitable, that he had known from the moment of the phone call today that this is what they had come here for, that he was doing no more than playing out the final scene in a play that was already fully scripted.

Lambert continued as though he hadn't spoken: 'Blackmail is an awful crime. As the victim, you would have had protection and a lot of sympathy. Your counsel will no doubt offer it as a mitigating circumstance, in due course. But you will be charged with murder, and the method you used was plainly premeditated rather than a spur of the moment action. There will be a mandatory life sentence, though it will be interesting to see what recommendations the judge will make about how long you should serve.'

It was almost like one of the solicitors Richard knew from Rotary, giving informed opinion about a case of the day. Richard wanted to join in, to put the case for mercy. He could scarcely believe that this was his own future which was at issue. Or his lack of a future.

With that thought, his pretensions towards resistance almost disappeared. He asked the token question, again feeling as though his part in this play demanded it. 'What makes you think I was being blackmailed?'

'You were always the likeliest candidate, once we had to account for that extra thousand in Kate Wharton's account.'

'You're suggesting that I murdered the girl for the sake of a paltry thousand pounds?'

Lambert smiled, more it seemed in sorrow than in anger. 'Blackmailers come back for more. We see it all the time. They may not even intend to as they make the first demand, but the money comes to them too easily, and they almost always go back to the well for more. It leads people into desperate actions to silence them, as it did in this case.'

'You've no evidence for this.'

'We wouldn't be here to arrest you if we didn't. We spoke to Tracey Boyd this morning. She admitted to demanding the sum of two thousand pounds from you.'

'Kate Wharton's flatmate.' Richard found it a small, incongruous satisfaction to have the identity he had guessed at confirmed.

'We know you drew that sum in cash from your bank yesterday. We could have let you take the money to her tomorrow night as arranged, but we didn't want another dead woman on our hands.'

It was over, now. It was a relief not to have to go on with his hopeless denials. 'I couldn't let Kate ruin everything. I liked her, felt I'd got to know her, over the months. Then she tried to blackmail me.'

'You should have come to us.'

Richard scarcely heard Bert Hook's first words. 'She said she was giving up the game, going away with her boyfriend to start anew somewhere else. She wanted more money quickly, to give them a start. She'd had her thousand, but then she came back with a demand for more.'

Lambert said with grim insistence, 'As DS Hook says, you should have come and asked for police help. You'd have had protection. The victim's identity is not reported, when a blackmail case is in court.'

'But she'd have told people, before it ever came to court. Told people at the golf club and at my firm. I'd have been a laughing stock where I at present have respect. I couldn't face that.' He glanced automatically at the ceiling, as a proper sense of priorities belatedly asserted itself. 'And Eileen would have found out. She doesn't deserve that.'

And now she would have to face all that and something much worse. The husband who had ministered so diligently to her increasing needs revealed as not just a man with a secret sexual life but as a murderer, a man who had planned and executed the cold-blooded garrotting of a girl with her life before her. Ellacott might be a man who had wandered out of his depth, but there was no escaping the reality of what he had done.

He now waved his fingers vaguely across the front of his hair, as if he felt some of it must surely be out of place, and asked wearily, 'What next?'

Lambert said evenly, 'We shall arrest you here. You will be formally charged with the murder of Katherine Mary Wharton at Oldford Police Station.'

He nodded slowly, then looked up into the superinten-dent's long, watchful face. 'You didn't come for me at first. There must have been others under suspicion as well as me. What put you on to me?'

Lambert shrugged. 'You made a mistake. Told us a lie. One you needn't have used, as a matter of fact. You said you hadn't played recently at the Ross-on-Wye course. The steward there told us yesterday that you were there quite recently. Three weeks ago, in fact: I checked the date of the match with the Secretary this morning. Just eleven days before the body of Kate Wharton was dumped in that ditch on the eleventh hole.'

Ellacott nodded three times, as if it gave him satisfaction to see things falling into place. 'I thought at the time that it would be a good place to dump a body. I must have already been feeling desperate.'

'And on Sunday the sixth of May you did just that.'

'Yes. Kate had come back with a demand for another two thousand four days earlier. Claimed it would be the last one, but she'd said that the first time. I decided I'd have to do something drastic. I said it would take me a few days to get the cash, but I knew I had to act by Sunday, because my car was already booked in for a service and a thorough valeting on the Monday, which would remove any traces of Kate Wharton from the upholstery before her body was even discovered. So I told her I'd pick her up in my car on Sunday evening, late on.'

'What time was this?'

'Ten fifteen, on a road near her flat. She was upset when she came, so she wasn't even suspicious. She said she'd had a row with this boyfriend. I'd taken a waxed cord from a sash window with me. I pointed to something outside the car window, and had the cord around her neck as soon as she turned away from me. She didn't make a sound. I couldn't believe it was so easy to kill someone. I drove out to the Ross course and turned down that lane which runs alongside the tenth and the eleventh fairways. If there'd been anyone around, I'd simply have driven on, but there wasn't.'

'You put things over your feet before you went through the hedge.'

'Yes. Just plastic bags from the supermarket, but they did the trick. You haven't produced anything from the site.'

'No. You didn't even leave fibres on the hedge, it seems.'

'I put on my golfing waterproof trousers so that I wouldn't. They went into the dustbin and off to the dump the next day.' He seemed proud of the precautions he had taken, anxious to confirm to himself that he had made only the one slip, in lying about his recent visit to the Ross golf course.

At a sign from Lambert, Hook moved forward and pronounced the words of arrest. Ellacott winced slightly at the iteration of the word murder, but was otherwise impassive. 'What now?' he asked.

'You must come with us to the station at Oldford. You will be placed under arrest and held there for the moment. You will be taken to court for an initial hearing quite soon.'

'I'll need to make arrangements for Eileen.'

'If you give us the name of a friend or a professional carer, Sergeant Hook will ask them to come here.'

He gave them a name and Hook made a careful, non-committal phone call. He set down the phone, looked at Ellacott with a troubled face, and said, 'She'll be over in half an hour.'

Ellacott went out between them into the hall and stopped suddenly there. 'I must tell Eileen. I can't let this come to her from others.'

Lambert hesitated. 'All right. It's irregular, but in the circumstances, we'll allow it. DS Hook will be watching the windows on that side of the house from outside and I'll stay here. We can allow you no more than five minutes.'

As he stood awkwardly to one side and Richard Ellacott went heavily up the stairs, John Lambert could not rid his mind of the thought that he still had almost three months left before retirement. Still time, perhaps, for a final murder investigation. But how could you hope that someone amidst those anonymous thousands out there would be planning such awful things?

Richard Ellacott hesitated for a moment on the landing, then went into his wife's bedroom and shut the door.

There would be hard moments for him to come, in court, and harsher times still, as a murderer in prison. But the worst nightmare of all was going on at this moment, behind that shut door in this quiet house.